CLAIMING HER BEASTS
BOOK ONE

DIA COLE

Claiming Her Beasts Book One

Published by Black Diamond Press LLC.

ISBN: 978-1-946975-28-7

AUTHOR'S NOTE

This story is based on my Heaven in Hell series, originally written in 2015. The series (along with most all of my books) takes place in a world reeling from a global pandemic where the eagerly awaited flu vaccine brings about the apocalypse. Despite what some of my readers have suggested, I'm not clairvoyant (I wish) and the fact that these fictional events mirror current world events is merely a coincidence. My stories are written purely for entertainment and are never intended to be taken as social, political, or medical commentary.

FYI: This steamy and thrilling ride is not for the faint of heart and some content may be triggering to sensitive readers.

SUMMARY

Family is everything and I'll do whatever it takes to support what's left of mine. I'll work double waitressing shifts seven days a week. I'll even become the headliner at the local strip club.

But I draw the line at accepting a drug lord's indecent proposal. I'm not for sale. Unfortunately, the monster isn't used to taking no for an answer and his ability to manipulate minds makes him a formidable enemy.

Luckily, I've got my sexy roommate and a dangerous shifter watching out for me. They'll protect me from everything... except their dark desires.

If I can survive these beasts, the apocalypse will be a cakewalk.

❧ I ❧

HUNTER

The humans in the strip club had no idea their world was ending. I didn't know whether to pity them or cheer on their impending doom.

The bleach-blonde cocktail waitress who was riding the hard edge of forty slopped a watered-down Jack and Coke on the table in front of me. "This is your fifth, Sly. You aren't driving anywhere tonight, right?"

I peered at her through the dark sunglasses that hid my inhuman eyes. "Nah, Donna." I slurred my words and swayed slightly in my seat.

"Good," she said absently, as if she gave a damn. From what I'd observed the past few weeks, neither Donna nor her fat club owner husband cared much for anything other than cold hard cash.

As long as I paid for the copious amounts of shitty alcohol I drank, they overlooked my shaggy hair, hooded trench coat, and apparent alcoholism.

Tossing back the drink, I sprawled in my chair and played the part of a drunk. Sweat dotted my forehead from the strain of keeping the small human form, but it wasn't anything I wasn't used to.

All my missions required me to suppress my natural scent and either make myself invisible—something I could only do for a short time—or shrink my normally massive body into an average human-sized one. As a result, bystanders never paid much attention to me.

Case in point. No one in the nearly empty strip club glanced twice at me. Not the beautiful dancer on the stage or the disabled vet that watched over her from the door. Not the former linebacker manning the bar or the jackass in a sweater vest seated at the table in front of me. And certainly not the mixture of human and shifter gang members speaking in low voices at the back of the club.

Those fuckers owed their lives to the chip implanted in my head. If freed from the oversight of my handler, I'd shift into the monstrous beast I was and shred them to pieces.

A magnificent vision of what that would look like had me hissing under my breath.

It'd been thirty-two days, six hours, and twenty-seven minutes since I'd been let off my leash, and bloodlust coiled inside me, dark and hungry.

My current handler often forgot killing was one of my biological imperatives, and she wasted my otherworldly abilities on tracking and spying.

But all work and no play makes Hunter a dull boy...

A low growl rumbled inside my chest. Thankfully, none of the humans could hear it over the sensual beat of the music pulsing through the club.

Javier Diaz, the Alpha I'd been sent to watch, might have detected the inhuman noise, if he'd bothered to tear his attention from the dark-haired female dancing on stage. He, like me, was a shifter with highly developed senses. By his scent, he was some kind of jungle cat. Jaguar. Leopard. Whatever the fuck he was, his slender bones would snap like kindling under my giant paws.

The beast inside me demanded I assert my dominance over him and his enforcers. None of them could come close to me in power and strength, and any territory I was in was mine by default. I ached to punish him and his enforcers for occupying the same space and daring to look at the female I desired.

I glanced briefly at the beautiful creature on the stage. The dancer's long brown hair fanned over her exquisite face as she twirled around the silver pole.

She'll be mine. Not his.

I bared my teeth, feeling my aggression rise. The blood-thirsty beast lurking under my skin didn't care that I was a military operative sent here to gather intel on Javier and his faction. All it cared about was killing and—

An intoxicating odor wafted from the stage, shifting my bloodlust into something else. Heat pooled low in my body and my cock hardened. The dancer's scent—creamy vanilla and female musk—fogged my mind and awoke long denied instincts.

Suddenly, it was impossible to focus on anything but the dancer. She undulated on stage wearing nothing but a G-string and white wings strapped to her back.

I reached into my pocket and pulled out one of the white feathers I'd found after a previous show. Keeping my face lowered, I brought it to my nose and inhaled deeply. My dancer's scent still clung to the downy fringe.

I groaned, my beast urging me to drop to the floor and roll around in the fragrance.

According to my sources, the owner of the feather was Heaven Lee Walker. Server by day. Exotic dancer by night. Human.

I inhaled deeply, branding her alluring scent into my mind and body. My sources were wrong.

She couldn't be entirely human if her scent called to me on this level.

What is she?

My highly acute senses detected no shifter blood. Nor was she any of the other abominations genetically engineered by the military. And yet, her scent called to me on a level nothing ever had before.

For the first time in my miserable existence, I wanted to claim a female. This female.

Weeks of inhaling her pheromones and watching her seductive dance night after night had aroused me to a dangerous level.

Venom pooled in my mouth as I tracked every one of her sinuous movements. *Pretty. So very pretty.*

Fuck. Pretty was an understatement.

Her curvaceous body was perfection by the standards of any species. Round hips. Heart-shaped ass. Breasts large enough to fill even my enormous hands.

Like me, Javier seemed unable to tear his gaze from her smooth golden skin and long toned legs that wrapped around the pole. The Alpha leaned forward, looking ready to pounce.

A warning growl escaped my lips.

If the other shifter made any move toward my dancer, it would be his last.

My dancer? Fuck. When did I start thinking of her as mine?

I shook my head as if to clear it. This assignment was getting the best of me. Maybe it was a good thing it would soon end.

With the coming apocalypse, the military would have more important things to worry about than the clandestine activities of a rogue shifter's faction. And they would reassign me to doing what I did best—killing.

But what will happen to my dancer when shit hits the fan?

I clenched the feather tighter in my fist before realizing I was crushing it. *Fuck.* I gently put the delicate plume back in my pocket.

I'd drawn out this mission for weeks so I could watch over my dancer as long as I could. She had grit, but not the fighting skills she'd need to survive what was coming.

The crippled old man who drove her home each night wasn't strong enough to protect her. Nor could that cocksucker roommate of hers, unless he grew a pair overnight.

When the end of humanity came, she'd die, like everyone else in this fucking town.

Unless I save her...

My twin brother, Ghost, used to say that opportunity came from chaos. Perhaps I could leverage the upcoming panic and mayhem to break free from my handler.

And maybe pigs can fly.

Sighing, I rubbed the back of my head. Until I figured out a way to remove my implant without killing myself, I was nothing more than a highly trained pet. One wrong move and my handler wouldn't hesitate to put me down.

But my dancer might be worth dying for...

Visions of my hands and mouth on her delectable body made my cock throb against the suddenly too-tight fabric of my pants.

"Hunter, your vitals are going haywire. What's going on?" a deep feminine voice asked through the tiny electronic device implanted in my inner ear.

I cursed under my breath. For a moment, I'd forgotten that my handler could sense my emotions and monitor my biometric readings. Jen could also give me orders I was compelled to follow and punish me if I displeased her. It was the military's way of leashing their most lethal weapon.

"It's that dancer, isn't it?" she said with a heavy sigh. The artificial link between us wasn't anywhere near as strong as the natural bonds I'd had with my brothers or the connection I'd had with my previous handler, but I could still feel echoes of her annoyance and frustration.

I grunted, unable to lie to her.

"You know the rules. Don't touch the humans," she warned.

Screw the rules.

Jen sighed again. "Your mating drive is spiking. We'll... find you a receptive female." Her voice grew tight and unease pulsed through our bond. She must have remembered what happened to the last breeder they tried to force on me.

"No." I'd never let that happen again.

"Then focus on the goddamn mission. Find out where Javier is keeping Dr. Hurran."

The mention of the army scientist who loved inflicting pain on her subjects made me clench my jaw. Javier could have the sadistic bitch.

"Hunter, are you listening? We need to find out where he is keeping her."

Why does it matter? Especially now, when the countdown to the end of days had begun.

"Surely, he's said something about her by now." Her desperation filtered through our bond.

"No. His conversations are all about deliveries and construction projects." *Disappointing, really.* You'd think the leader of the biggest cartel in the northern hemisphere would have more interesting things to discuss. "Not once has he mentioned the scientist."

Jen cursed. "We're running out of time. The Colonel is about to pull the plug on this operation."

My breathing went shallow. I knew what that meant. Humanity was running out of time. My dancer was running out of time.

"So, stop dicking around and find out where he is keeping the scientist."

"By any means necessary?" Excitement thrummed through me as I waited for Jen to respond. If she let me loose, I'd have the information in less than five minutes. Of course, Javier and his crew wouldn't survive the interrogation, but that was no great loss.

"You know our orders. Do not approach the target or his enforcers," she said, sounding as tired of this shit as I was.

Which fuck nut desk jockey made that rule? How was I supposed to get critical intel from the leader of a rogue shifter faction without cracking a few skulls?

"Just get the intel and be back at base by zero four hundred hours."

"Why?" The strip club didn't close until four.

"Because I said so." The frost in Jen's voice made it clear she didn't owe me an explanation.

"Ten-four." I tried for a more agreeable tone. It was never a good idea to piss off the person who could unleash gut-wrenching pain with the click of a button.

There was a long pause, as if she was debating telling me something. "The Colonel ordered Dominic's release," she finally said in an unnaturally quiet voice.

Air rushed from my lungs. "What the fuck? He was in for life." My previous handler deserved to die a miserable death in prison for what he'd done. A blowtorch of fury blew through me. My hands shook as the pain-filled screams of my brothers echoed in my mind. "Dom can't be released."

"The Colonel wants all hands on deck," she said, trying to sound calm. Through our bond, I could feel how rattled she was. For some asinine reason, she loved Dom. Not that the ice-cold bastard was capable of returning the sentiment.

I took a deep steadying breath, trying to keep from exploding. *It's a good thing Dom's out. He'll be a lot easier to kill.*

"The Colonel wants to pair you two again," Jen added.

"N-no fucking way," I sputtered. I couldn't end Dom's life if they bound me to him.

"So, you'd prefer to stay with me then?"

I grunted, knowing full well the Colonel could give two shits about my preference. My fate was his to fuck with.

"Then I won't let them re-pair you," she said with so much conviction, the tension left my body. Jen had pull with the Colonel and although she and I had only been linked a short time, she was a soldier of her word. *Unlike Dom...*

Betrayer. Liar. Killer.

"I'll get the location of the scientist," I promised. I had to at least do that much for her considering I was going to murder her husband the first chance I got.

"Good. Don't blow your cover and remember the rules. Don't touch any humans."

As she severed our connection, it occurred to me the rules didn't apply to my dancer.

Because Lee's not entirely human, is she?

As I considered the potential loophole, the jackass at the table in front of me held up several crumpled bills.

My dancer prowled across the stage toward him. Her hips swayed seductively back and forth, and her jeweled navel ring caught the light and shimmered.

A whine caught in the back of my throat. I liked shiny things. A lot...

Fuck. I had to think of a way to complete the mission and get up close and personal with her... at least long enough to explore this hold she had over me.

Is she the one female that can tame my beast, or will it destroy her like all the others?

❦   2   ❦

LEE

Dance music shook the stage as I spun around the pole in my G-string. A few rogue feathers from the wings strapped to my back floated gently to the body glitter-encrusted floor. Following them down, I crawled on my hands and knees over to the middle-aged man waving dollar bills in the air.

The rumpled off-the-rack tweed vest he wore told me he was likely one of the professors from the Southern Arizona University campus down the street.

Disappointing. He wouldn't have deep pockets like some of my big tippers. But beggars couldn't be choosers. Especially tonight.

Other than the professor, there were only a handful of other patrons in the strip club—Sly, a regular who came for the booze not the boobs, several dark-haired men talking quietly in the back corner, and Uncle Duncan. Since finding out the club bouncers had been laid off, the cowboy-hat-wearing grizzly old vet had come to every one of my shows. My surrogate uncle, always quick to spot trouble, never took his eyes off the dark-haired men deep in conversation.

The men's menacing vibe made me glad they sat far from the stage. They'd started meeting at Eros a few weeks ago. Max, my boss, was either too desperate for business or too scared to make them leave.

Truth be told, the guys dressed in black with gang tattoos creeping past their collars didn't rattle me as much as the elegant man sitting in the center of them. Javier Diaz was rumored to run one of the largest drug cartels in the Southwest. His gang, the Calaveras, was renowned for their violence and brutality.

Pity.

Even if he wasn't wearing a three-thousand-dollar suit, Javier would be one amazing-looking man. He wasn't as large as some of the men seated around him, but he radiated power. Tonight, his shoulder-length hair was tied back, emphasizing high cheekbones, full lips, and startling amber eyes. Those incredible eyes studied my body as I danced.

I shivered, feeling caught in the stare of a predator. Trying to ignore the striking man, I focused on the professor. Based on the flush in his cheeks, he'd had more than the two-drink minimum.

Good for me. Bad for his bank account. I cupped my bare breasts and lifted them for his perusal.

He licked his lips and handed me a wad of bills.

I tucked them into my G-string as I undulated my hips. What was it about guys and breasts? They seemed to lose all reason when a pair was flashed their way.

It was the same with the professor. His pupils dilated, and he swallowed hard. He rubbed his mouth with one trembling hand while reaching for his wallet with the other.

Excellent. I purred my approval. I caressed my inner thighs, making seductive promises with my heavy-lidded gaze. *For this moment, I'll be your woman.*

Of course, it was just an act, I'd never belong to any man.

But he didn't need to know that. I slipped my fingers into my G-string and snapped the elastic band.

He gasped, his eyes glazed with lust.

Donna sidled up next to him, adjusting the crooked Santa hat clipped to her badly dyed blonde hair. "Want another drink?"

The professor tore his gaze from me.

The spell was broken.

I glared at Donna.

As if realizing her mistake, she gave me an apologetic look and mouthed "Sorry, Lee." Given the dark shadows under her eyes, she probably hadn't slept in weeks. And no wonder. She'd lost her son to the canine flu a few months back and had never really recovered. I forgave her immediately. I knew all too well the pain of losing loved ones.

The song ended. Max, clutching a mic in his thick hands, hoofed it to the stage. "Give it up for our gorgeous heavenly creature. You can get a taste of Heaven every Thursday, Friday, and Saturday night. Up next, Mistress Robin will whip you into shape."

Uncle Duncan tipped his hat, motioned to the parking lot, and limped out the door. Sly slumped over his table. Javier raised his cognac glass in my direction while his men continued to ignore me. At least the professor clapped wildly.

Another piss-poor night.

Trying to hide my disappointment, I blew a kiss to the professor, gathered up the lingerie I'd scattered around the stage, and exited through the back curtains.

Havana, encased in silver-studded black latex, was preparing to go on. "Is it dead out there?"

"Stone-cold. Damn holidays." I couldn't wait for Christmas to be over. Not only did it hurt business, but the holiday season always reminded me of dark times I'd rather forget.

She sighed. "It's been bad since the canine flu hit."

No argument there. Not only had the worldwide pandemic killed off a quarter of the population, it'd also wreaked havoc on businesses everywhere. "Things will get better with the vaccine." All anyone talked about were the free shots that had just been rolled out to the public. I hadn't had time to wait in the huge lines to get mine yet.

"Took 'em long enough. Damn, if things around here don't pick up soon, I might have to start nannying again."

I smiled at the image of the BDSM queen looking after kids.

She adjusted one of the straps on her thigh-high stiletto boots. "What will you do?"

My mind blanked.

What will I do? I had to take care of my family. My waitressing gig wasn't paying much these days, and it wasn't as if high school dropouts had a lot of options. I still had a little money stashed away from better times.

But that won't get us far.

Techno music blared from the speakers out front.

Havana uncoiled her whip. "That's my cue."

Nodding goodbye, I headed to the dressing area. A thick cloud of coconut-scented body spray hung over the narrow room. Six makeup vanity mirrors competed for space with the rows of lockers behind them. I waved to Cami, who was doing her makeup in the back, and made my way to my chair.

I started to sit but thankfully remembered to unstrap my wings before I crushed them. Those damn things cost a pretty penny, not that I didn't have a backup pair. I glanced in the mirror at the black tattoo of angel wings that covered my back from the tops of my shoulders to the base of my spine. Getting inked hurt like a bitch, but it was a fitting tribute to the older sister I'd lost.

I hung the fluffy white wings on a nearby hook and

collapsed into my chair. After kicking off my stilettos, I rubbed my feet and tried to remember a time when they didn't ache.

A naked pair of double Ds brushed my cheek.

Seriously? I glared up at the tiny blonde woman standing over me. "Get your tits out of my face, Cami."

She laughed and took a step back. "Jealous?"

I raised a brow.

"Okay. I'm the jealous one. You have a better rack and you didn't even have to pay for it."

I reached into my G-string, pulled out the crumpled one-dollar bills, and slapped them on the counter. "Fat lot of good they did me tonight. Twenty bucks, and I didn't pull in much more at my shift at Hooters. At this rate, I won't make rent."

Her forehead furrowed. "You know, you could always join me doing escort work. You'd make great money."

Not this again. I rolled my eyes.

"Don't give me that look. You don't have to do anything you don't want to do. It's not like we're hookers or anything."

I raised my brow again.

"Fine. If you want to make the good money, you do a few... things. Men would pay top dollar to pop that cherry of yours. I'm talking four or five Gs, baby girl."

I rested my head on my hands.

Is this what it has come to? Bartering my virginity?

I felt Cami's hand on my shoulder. "You look tired. Forget I said anything." She paused. "Have you seen the news?"

"No. Why?"

The fact that she didn't say anything right away was clue enough that something was up. I lifted my gaze to meet her cornflower blue eyes in the mirror. "Why, Cami?"

She fiddled with the tiny plaid skirt she wore. "Best Friends staged a rally earlier tonight."

At the mention of my sister's animal rights group, my

stomach tightened. "Eden said they were just meeting for coffee."

Cami set her bubblegum-pink, gem-encrusted cell phone down on the counter in front of me. A video from the local news station played.

I peered into the tiny screen.

A distinguished-looking male reporter cleared his throat. "Around the country reports of canine flu vaccine reactions are emerging. At least twenty deaths have been linked to the long-awaited vaccine, and several hospitals, including our own Saguaro Valley General, have reported bizarre cannibalistic behavior among a subset of recently vaccinated. The Food and Drug Administration along with the Centers for Disease Control and Prevention have denied the vaccine has played any role in these—"

Cami snatched her phone. "Holy crap. I got my vaccine earlier today. Oh, my God. I thought the injection site looked weird. Does it look strange to you?" She held up her left arm. Colorful tattoos covered it from shoulder to wrist.

I scoffed. "Like I can see anything under all that ink."

She poked at her skin. "It feels numb, and I swear there are a bunch of black veins there. I never should've let my sister blackmail me into getting that vaccine. Everyone knows vaccines are full of toxic chemicals. Just the other day I saw a post that said—"

"Enough with your conspiracy theories." I tugged the phone back and pressed the play button. The video continued.

"And in local news, an animal rights group clashed with police at the Canine Memorial Fountain in Heritage Square earlier this evening. The group, Best Friends for Life, has been vocal in protesting Order 1537—the law requiring all dogs be euthanized to stop the spread of the deadly canine flu."

Behind the reporter, footage played of police in riot gear closing in on a group of screaming people.

Something in the corner of the screen caught my eye.

I paused the video and stared at the image of my sister standing on the edge of the fountain.

Dammit. The brat is even wearing my jacket.

Eden's dark brown hair flew around her oval face as she held up a sign that read 'Don't Kill Our Fur Babies.'

I felt the blood drain out of my face. "She promised she wouldn't do this again."

I'd spent more money bailing her out of jail over the past few months than I had on our grocery bills. My thumb must've brushed the play button because the reporter continued, "All protesters were arrested, and no injuries were reported. Only ten more shopping days left until Christm—"

I ended the video and looked into Cami's sympathetic gaze. "Goddamn it. I'm going to kill her."

"Give her a break. She's young."

"She's only two years younger than we are. I'm so tired of her bullshit. She spends all her time on this stupid animal rights crap and hasn't bothered to go on even one of the job interviews I've set up for her. Not that she's likely to get any offers with her growing rap sheet." I let out a deep breath. "Can I make a call?"

"Didn't you finally get your own phone?"

I felt my cheeks flush. "I don't know where it is."

Likely my kleptomaniac of a sister helped herself to it like she did all my stuff.

Not that I'd really cared. It'd taken both Cami and Reed begging me to get with the twenty-first century before I'd agreed to get a cell phone in the first place. As a self-proclaimed technophobe, I just didn't see the point.

"Sure. I gotta finish my face or I'll scare the men off."

I scoffed. "Shut up. You know you're gorgeous." I wasn't

exaggerating. The petite woman was a walking Barbie doll. Her light skin and blonde hair were a stark contrast to my dark coloring.

"That's why you're my best friend, sugar. You're great for the ego." Smiling, she sashayed over to her chair.

Having long ago memorized the non-emergency line, I quickly dialed the police station.

The line was busy.

That's odd.

Deciding that finding my sister was an emergency, I called 9-1-1.

It was busy too.

What the hell? Don't dispatchers answer all emergency calls?

Ending the call, I dialed Reed's cell phone.

"Yaaallo," said the voice on the other line.

"Reed?" I asked, momentarily taken aback.

"Nah. This is the Ron Meister, baby. You sound hot. You should come over and party with us."

I could barely hear him over the sound of raucous laughter and music. My blood simmered. "Ronnie, this is Lee. Put Reed on now."

It sounded as if the phone dropped.

"Ronnie," I shouted.

I heard him curse and yell, "Turn the music down."

"Oh. Ah. Sorry about that, Lee. I'll get him right now."

My spiking blood pressure didn't allow me to enjoy the nervousness in his tone.

"Lee," said a deep, velvety voice a moment later.

"Reed, tell me you didn't let your stupid band friends throw another party at our house."

I heard him catch his breath. "It's just a small shindig."

Small, my ass.

It sounded as though half the neighborhood was at the house. "Reed. We've been over this. The landlord said no more parties. Besides, you know how I feel about Ronnie." The arrogant lead singer of Reed's band had tried to hit on me one too many times. The last time he tried to feel me up I'd kicked him in the balls so hard, he'd sung soprano for a week.

"Ronnie thought we should celebrate my birthday," Reed said in an apologetic tone.

Crap. I'd totally forgotten. My chair seemed to sink two feet into the floor. "Reed, I'm so sorry. I didn't mean to..."

"It's okay. You've been pulling double shifts all week. I think you might even forget your name at this point." His laugh was hollow. "But you won't have to work so hard soon. I know one of these interviews is going to pan out."

I pinched the bridge of my nose. Reed had been desperately trying to find work since being laid off from the coffee shop. With unemployment at record highs, jobs were in short supply these days. "I know you'll find something soon. How about tomorrow I take you out for a nice birthday dinner?"

Assuming I have any money left after bailing Eden's ass out of jail.

"You don't have to do that. It's not like turning twenty is any big deal. I'll have everybody out by the time you get home."

Guilt swamped me. "No. Let them stay. Celebrate with your friends. But don't go crazy with the drinking. Okay?"

"Really?" His voice brightened.

"Just this once. Hey, have you heard from Eden?"

His silence was damning.

"Reed."

He let out a sigh. "She got arrested again. She called me from jail to ask if I'd pick her up after her court appearance tomorrow morning. She didn't want you to find out."

"That little..." My fingernails curled into the armrest of my chair.

Max strode into the dressing room and motioned at me. The strained look on his sweaty face wasn't comforting.

My heart pounded. "Reed, I gotta go. Happy birthday."

I hung up the phone and looked up at my boss. "What is it?"

Please don't let him fire me. I need this job.

Max rubbed the top of his balding head. "Mr. Diaz wants to see you."

3

REED

"Lee?" Trying to filter out the loud music and drunken laughter around me, I pressed my phone into my ear. But she was gone.

The knowledge that I'd once again disappointed the one woman I wanted to impress was a knife twist into my gut. *What was I thinking?* I knew Lee was exhausted and near her breaking point.

For months she'd been pulling double and sometimes triple shifts, trying to scrape enough money together to keep a roof over our heads.

Through the cloud of cannabis smoke, I zeroed in on Ronnie's flushed face. Like always, he'd talked me into something I'd regretted. You'd think I'd have learned my lesson from all the other times he'd burned me. Like when I'd let him cheat off my test in chemistry class and we'd both gotten suspended. Or when I'd loaned him my brand-new speaker. I'd worked months of overtime to buy it, and he'd destroyed it in a single night.

Seeming to sense my glare, my drunk friend looked over at me. "What did the ball breaking bitch say?"

I rarely allowed myself to get angry, but I saw red. "Don't disrespect her." No one talked about Lee like that in front of me.

Ronnie must've sensed the change in my mood because he took a step back. "I meant, what did the beautiful Ms. Walker have to say?"

His change in tone popped my rage balloon. "She's fine with the party."

"Woohoo! We're going to party all night!" Ronnie whirled around in a circle. The quick movement sent his drunk ass off balance and he crashed into a stunning brunette who was talking to our friend Dexter.

"Hey!" she cried. Jungle juice splashed over the top of her cup and ran down her chest as she pushed Ronnie away.

Ronnie leered at her. "Want me to lick that off you?"

She cringed and moved closer to Dexter.

"I'm the lead singer of Panorama." Ronnie motioned around the room where Morgan and Sam were setting up their musical equipment. "We're getting signed by a record label this week. Soon we'll be famous, and you'll tell all your friends about me."

"Right," she said, rolling her heavily kohled eyes. The sarcasm in her voice made me think of Lee.

Lee also didn't believe Panorama was ever going to amount to anything. But Ronnie wasn't lying.

Three days ago, our band met with Topic Records. One of their execs had seen us open for Blue Puppy and he'd sent his people to track us down.

The label was legit offering to sign us. It was only a one-off deal, and the percentage of royalties weren't anything to cream our jeans over, but it was a motherfucking contract. *Our big break.* It was everything we'd been dreaming about since we first started jamming together.

But Ronnie had read somewhere never to take a first offer, and in his infinite idiocy had told Topic Records we'd think it over. *What the hell is there to think about?* Someone wanted to pay us to make music. Up to this point we'd been playing for free drinks and the occasional tip crammed into a collection cup.

So eager to sign so I'd have some money to offer Lee, I'd nearly strangled Ronnie with the strap of my bass guitar. But then Sam and Morgan started saying they were having second thoughts about 'selling out to the man,' and I realized it would never happen.

Panorama would never be a household name. We'd never play stadiums. The songs I'd written would never be sung by anyone other than our most devoted fans. And worst of all, I'd never make enough money through music to keep the woman I loved from selling her body on stage every night.

I tightened my fingers around my phone as the familiar feelings of frustration and shame washed over me. *What kind of man doesn't help support his family?*

I imagined I could hear the ghostly echo of my mom's voice in my head saying, *"Don't be like your deadbeat dad."*

My shoulder's sagged as I struggled to bring to mind the face of the rock band roadie I'd only met a handful of times. I wouldn't be like that guy. I wouldn't chase a career in music at the expense of my family.

And so earlier today, I'd finally manned up. I'd pawned my bass. It was an unfortunate twist of irony that my mom had given it to me on this day six years ago. But nostalgia wouldn't pay the rent.

I slid my phone into my back pocket and felt for the fat wad of cash there. I couldn't wait to see the look on Lee's face when she saw the money. Just imagining her reaction made me smile. Maybe I could talk her into going out with me somewhere. Just the two of us. Like a date...

As I slipped into the fantasy of Lee and me together, the brunette gave me a coy smile.

"Who's your hot friend?" she asked Dexter loudly.

The annoyed look on my friend's face made me wince. Dexter hated it when the girls he liked went after me. I'd like to say it was a rare occurrence, but it wasn't.

Ronnie interjected, "That's Reed, but don't waste your time. He's been in love with the same girl his entire life."

"Aw," the brunette said, her smile softening. "That's sweet."

Dexter scoffed. "Nah, it's fucking tragic. She doesn't return his feelings."

I turned away before I could see the brunette's expression turn to pity. I didn't need anyone's sympathy. Lee didn't love me the way I loved her... yet. But I knew she would one day.

She was the one for me. I'd known it the moment she'd saved me from those older boys who were bullying me the first day of kindergarten.

One minute I was being shoved into the dirt. The next minute an avenging angel had rushed over from the bus stop. Baring her teeth like a rabid wolf, Lee had rounded on the older boys. "Why don't you pick on someone your own size?" She'd lifted her fists in a clear invitation.

Although she was much smaller than they were, the boys took off running.

She'd glared after them, and then helped me to my feet. *"They won't bother you now that you're with me."*

And from that moment forward, I was with her. She'd owned my heart and soul. I'd followed her everywhere. Over time, she and Eden became my best friends and their Gran became my second mother.

The sound of Morgan tuning his electric guitar tore me from my memories.

Sam sat down at his drums and pounded out a frenetic

beat I felt in the marrow of my bones. The ache to play with them was almost physically painful.

Moving closer, I took a seat on Gran's lumpy old couch just across from Morgan's amp. Even years after her death, the lingering scent of Gran's Shalimar perfume still clung to the polyester cushions. The smell brought to mind happier times. Times when Eden, Lee, Gran, and I had gathered in the living room of the old house and played games or watched some mindless show on television.

Morgan flipped his long hair out of his face and scowled at me. I wasn't sure if he was pissed at me for quitting the band or if he was just in a foul mood.

Trying to ignore his glare, I struck imaginary chords on my knee. *Damn.* Losing my bass and my band hurt worse than I'd imagined. Maybe one of these lame ass jobs I kept interviewing for would pan out and I'd make enough money to buy my bass back.

My mind drifted back to the interview I'd had this afternoon. The convenience store manager had stared at my long hair in barely disguised disgust.

Screw that guy. Lee liked my hair, and I wouldn't change anything about my appearance that she admired. Hell, just look what I'd been willing to go through earlier this year for her. Memories of the weeks of throbbing pain had me shifting uncomfortably in my seat.

The cushions next to me dipped.

I glanced over to see the gorgeous brunette sitting next to me.

"Ronnie said to give you this." She offered me a cup of jungle juice.

I glanced over her shoulder.

Ronnie and Dexter were standing in the hallway. Ronnie motioned between me and the brunette while dry humping the air. Dexter gave him a sour look and stormed into the kitchen.

"When a beautiful woman offers you a drink, you take it," the brunette admonished.

Amused at her boldness, I grabbed the red cup and took a sip. All I tasted was the sugary Kool-Aid, which was impressive because I knew Ronnie had dumped at least eight bottles of alcohol into the mix.

The brunette smiled, her teeth flashing white against her dark lipstick. "I'm Aubry."

"I'm Reed."

"I know." She continued staring at me the way the band groupies did. Like they wanted to spray whip cream all over me and eat me for dessert.

"My friend Dexter is into you," I said, motioning toward the kitchen with my free hand.

"But I'm into you."

Shit.

"Whoa, those are some scars."

I looked down, horrified to see that my shirt cuff had ridden up, exposing my wrist tattoos and the web of mangled flesh of my forearm. Cursing under my breath, I quickly yanked the fabric down.

"Don't be self-conscious, I think your scars are cool. I have some of my own." She rolled down the top of her black fingerless gloves, revealing horizontal scars lining her forearm from wrist to elbow. "I used to be a cutter. How did you get yours?"

I shifted uneasily. "A car accident." Hoping she wouldn't dig any deeper, I gulped down the rest of the jungle juice and pulled out a pack of cloves. "Mind if I smoke?"

It was kind of ridiculous to ask her permission since it technically was my house, but my mom had drummed politeness into me.

"Of course not. Can I bum one?"

"Sure." As soon as I handed her a clove and lit it, she took a long drag.

"Damn, that's good."

I made a non-committal sound, enjoying the spiced cigarette. A hit from the bong in the kitchen would have been better, but Lee wasn't a fan of pot, so I was trying to cut down.

Aubry took a drag of her clove and leaned back against the couch cushions.

I tried not to notice her ample cleavage, but it was kind of hard with her low-cut corset.

Lee had a few tops like that she wore for her shows. Sometimes she was so tired she didn't bother changing, and I got a chance to see her in them.

My dick hardened as I remembered how incredible she'd looked wearing that black leather one. One day, when we were together, I'd ask her to wear that one for me... and only me.

Aubry let out a husky laugh and ran her hand over her chest. "Like what you see?"

With a start, I realized I was full on staring at her tits and my boner was obvious. Embarrassed, I choked on a mouthful of smoke.

Seeming amused at my coughing fit, Aubry smiled. "Ronnie said this was your place."

"Yeah." I was surprised he didn't call it his place as often as he crashed here.

"He also said it was your birthday."

I shrugged. Birthdays weren't really a big deal. Not when Lee forgot most of them.

Aubry cocked her head to the side as if she was waiting for me to say more.

I noticed her irises were pale green.

Eyes like desert sage... That might be a good lyric in the song I was working on. I glanced around for the pad of paper I always kept handy.

Eyes like desert sage. Fill with rage...

Nah, that didn't work. *Eyes like desert sage. Imprisoning me in a cage... Hmm.* It had potential.

Unable to find my pad and paper, I pulled out my phone and started texting myself.

Aubry pursed her lips. "Is there someone else you'd rather talk to?"

"Nah. I just thought of a line to a song."

"Yeah?" Aubry leaned over to look at my screen. When she saw what I'd written, she grinned. "Is that about me?"

"Kind of." I wished she'd go bother someone else. Dexter would probably give his left nut to be sitting this close to her. I opened my mouth to tell her so, but she pressed her lips against my ear.

"I'd like to imprison you in a cage." She bit down.

"Ah!" I jerked away, my earlobe stinging. "Why did you do that?"

She gave me a smoldering look. "What fun is pleasure without pain?"

Shit. I was clearly out of my depth with this woman.

Laughing, Aubry blew a smoke ring around my head. Then, flicking the rest of her clove into my empty cup, she stood and reached for my hand. "How about you show me your room and I'll let you bite me back."

4

LEE

My breath came out in a quick gasp. *Javier wants to see me?* In all the weeks he and his men had been coming to Eros, he'd never asked to meet any of the dancers. Of course, he never looked at the other dancers the way he looked at me.

Cami swiveled around in her chair. "You're not planning on pimping Lee out to the drug lord, are you?"

Max jerked as though she'd punched him in the solar plexus and rubbed his hands together nervously. "No. Nothing like that. He just wants to meet her, okay? I don't like it either, but money is tight. We need his business."

I don't need that kind of business.

I stood up and headed toward the lockers. "I've already done two sets. I'm off the clock. Besides, my ride is waiting." I couldn't keep Uncle Duncan sitting in the parking lot all night.

"Please, Lee." Max tugged at his candy-cane striped tie as if it was strangling him.

I sighed in resignation. "Okay, but I'm not doing any lap dances."

He bobbed his head up and down so fast, his jowls shook. "And I'm skipping my first set tomorrow."

It wasn't as if I'd make any money with the early set, anyway.

His eyes narrowed. "Friday's our biggest night and you're our headliner."

"I'll be there for my ten o'clock." I slid my heels back on, trying to ignore the protest made by my feet. "Look, do you want me to meet Javier or not?"

He threw his hands up in the air. "Fine."

Cami grabbed my arm as I followed Max to the doorway. Her face pinched with worry.

"Be careful. Javier Diaz is a dangerous man."

Great. If Cami, notorious for her less than stellar taste in men, was worried, Javier had to be really bad news.

My stomach became a writhing ball of snakes. "I'll be fine. I left your phone on my chair." I gently tugged away from her. "There's a party at the house tonight for Reed's birthday. If you're not doing anything after your set, why don't you swing by?"

Her heart-shaped face brightened. "That'd be fun. Maybe I'll give that sexy birthday boy a present he won't ever forget." She winked.

Something inside me balked at her interest in Reed, but before I could analyze my feelings, Max threw us an aggravated look.

"Come on, Lee. Time is money. Cami, have you seen Jess?"

I couldn't hide the revulsion on my face. The auburn-haired stripper had made my life a living hell ever since Max gave me her time slot and moved her sets later.

Cami shared a knowing look with me. "No evil-bitch-of-the-West sightings here, Max. When are you going to fire her ass? Last week, Jess poured baby oil all over the stage steps, Havana hurt her back, and Lee nearly broke her leg."

Remembering the nasty fall I'd taken made me wince.

Jess's mean-spirited pranks were going to get me killed one of these days.

"I don't know why you ladies can't just get along. Hurry up, Lee." Max huffed out of the room.

So much for his begging and pleading act. I hurried to catch up with my boss.

Max was uncharacteristically quiet as we walked backstage and took the side stairs down. It added to my nervousness.

Javier seemed to inspire fear in everyone around him.

What did a man like that want from me?

My stomach churned as we moved through the dark hallway, past the VIP rooms, and out into the main club.

Onstage Havana was in her element. She'd shed her bodysuit and undulated to the throbbing beat of the music in nothing but a black G-string and her boots. Her whip was wrapped around the professor. Based on the dazed expression on his face, he'd just found his new religion.

Good for her.

My gaze skipped past the Christmas-light-encrusted bar and garland-wrapped faux Roman pillars to the back of the club. As I suspected, Javier watched my approach with the same intensity he watched my dancing. Some kind of primitive fight-or-flight instinct kicked in and I wanted to run. My knees trembled as I forced myself to walk toward him.

"Come on," Max said, grabbing my wrist and pulling me forward. When we got to Javier's table, Max cleared his throat. "Good evening, gentlemen. This is Heaven."

Unwilling to meet Javier's forceful gaze, I glanced at the men around him. They were dark-eyed with short dark hair except for the younger-looking man sitting closest to Javier. He had to be Javier's brother or cousin. The resemblance between the two men was striking, although the younger man's glossy dark hair was longer, falling free to the middle of his back. His eyes were also darker than Javier's and they heated as he slid out of the booth.

"You always had good taste in women, *Mano*." The long-haired man prowled around me like a shark circling an injured seal. "What a beauty you are, *señorita*. And such gorgeous hair." As he grabbed a lock of my hair, his ring-covered hand brushed against the top of my breast.

I reared back.

Max reacted immediately, stepping between us. "Sorry, no touching allowed."

Giving Max a look that froze the blood in my veins, the long-haired man slowly opened his hand, freeing my hair. "What fun is there in only looking?"

Javier jumped up, his hands fisted. "Luis, apologize immediately." The barely contained rage in his tone made me flinch.

Luis blanched and stepped away from me. "*Los siento, señorita*. I meant no offense."

Max moved aside, putting me eye to eye with Javier.

Even from two feet away, I could feel the power and coiled energy emanating from him. This wasn't a man to be trifled with. I suddenly remembered the rumors of how he enjoyed torturing his enemies before killing them. I had to clasp my hands together to stop them from shaking.

Javier smiled at me, calling my attention to the sharpness of his even white teeth. "Please ignore my brother. He has no manners." He glared at Luis and the other men at the table. "Leave us."

Without a word, the men stood and walked toward the bar.

Javier gave Max a pointed look.

"Ah, I should introduce the next set," Max said, turning and heading for the stage.

I gritted my teeth. *Coward.* Max was getting a piece of my mind the next time we spoke.

"Please sit." Javier gestured toward the booth.

Seeing no other option, I scooted in.

Javier sank into the seat across from me. He was close enough that every breath I took was scented in the exotic spice of his expensive cologne.

"My name is Javier Diaz. I'm a great admirer of your dancing," he said with a faint accent.

"Thank you. I'm Heaven." Too late, I remembered Max had already introduced me. My face warmed. It wasn't like me to be frazzled.

"A pleasure to meet you." He extended his hand.

Once again, I saw no other option but to accept his handshake.

His long, warm fingers curled around mine. He lifted my hand to his lips and kissed my knuckles.

The sensation of his warm breath on my skin gave me goose bumps. I tried to pull away.

He refused to let me go.

I glanced up to see if Max was watching. Of course not. And my uncle had already left.

I'm on my own.

I broke out in a cold sweat.

Javier stroked one long finger over my palm, making me shiver.

"It's rare I'm so captivated by a female. From the first moment I saw you, I knew you were meant for me."

The vinyl seat stuck to my clammy skin as I shifted uneasily. Normally, at this point I'd be channeling my seductive alter ego, trying to work the guy for tips. But no part of me wanted to encourage this man. Just last week, Javier's last girlfriend had been found scalped and dismembered. A tremor slid down my spine.

"I'm having a private event at my home Saturday evening. I'd like you to attend."

I shook my head. Even if I wanted to rub shoulders with gangsters, going out with patrons was strictly against club rules. "I'm sorry, I'm working, and I'm not allowed to—"

"I've already spoken with Max. He said it'd be fine. You'll be well compensated for your time."

My mouth fell open in shock. *How could Max put me in this position?* Forgetting my fear for a moment, I glared at Javier. "I'm not a call girl."

"Of course not." He sat up straight as if I'd insulted him. "All you'd be asked to do is dance as you do here at the club. I'll pay twenty thousand for the evening."

My mouth went dry. Twenty thousand dollars. *Holy crap.* That'd keep Eden, Reed, and me afloat for months. *There has to be a catch.* "How many people would be at this event?"

His gaze heated and flickered to my bare breasts. "Just me."

Okayyyy. I swallowed hard. The room seemed to spin. This was one of those life-changing moments. I could feel it. If I chose to go down this road, there'd be no going back. I wasn't a fool. Javier didn't want to see me dance. He wanted to possess me. And not just for the night.

Am I willing to put my life on the line and sell what little is left of my soul?

Javier stroked his thumb over my wrist with way too much familiarity. "I'd pay double if you stayed through Sunday."

Double? Forty thousand dollars? My heart pounded faster than the beat of Havana's music. *How can I turn that down?*

"I would never ask you to do anything you didn't want to do." His voice deepened. "Look at me, *cariño*."

I lifted my gaze and was snared by his amber eyes.

"I know you're untouched."

I blinked in surprise. *How can he possibly know that?*

"But you're filled with desire. You need to be touched and pleasured." His voice rang with a strange tone that reverberated inside my head.

Inexplicably heat pooled between my legs.

Javier continued. "You're attracted to me. You want me. Don't you?"

Suddenly, I did want Javier.

"Answer me, *cariño*," he ordered in that strange voice.

Something made me blurt out, "Yes."

"Good. Very good." His silky voice was almost a purr. "Come close—"

He was interrupted by Max grabbing the mic and announcing the end of Havana's set.

I shook my head, feeling dazed and weirdly turned on. *What time is it? Uncle Duncan is probably freezing to death in the parking lot.*

I yanked my hand away from Javier. "I'll have to think your offer over." Before he could grab me again, I slid out of the booth.

The flash of anger in his gaze told me he wasn't used to being put off. He pushed something across the table. "Call me."

Blinking, I stared down at the shimmering black metal card.

Are those genuine diamonds embedded around the phone number?

"Thank you for your time." He reached into his wallet, pulled out several hundred-dollar bills and placed them on top of the card.

Part of me wanted to turn my back and walk away, sending the message I couldn't be bought. But the other part of me that was suddenly aching for his touch and desperate to keep my family afloat had me stuttering, "Th-thank you," while I grabbed the card and cash.

As if telepathically summoned, Javier's men left the bar and headed in our direction.

"Lee, don't keep me waiting. I'm not a patient man." Javier's tone held a note of warning.

It was suddenly hard to breathe.

He knows my real name. What else does he know about me?

Answering my unspoken question, he said, "Even though you live just down the street, I want Nero to drive you home." He motioned to a dangerous-looking man wearing a black suit.

Nero flashed me a dazzling smile.

It took me a second to realize that every single tooth in his mouth was gold plated.

I backed away on shaky legs. "No. I've got a ride, thank you."

"As you wish. I'll be looking forward to your call tomorrow, and to our date Saturday night."

I inwardly shuddered at the possessive gleam in his eyes. Clearly, in his mind, me agreeing to Saturday night was already a forgone conclusion. Turning my back on him, I sprinted toward the safety of the dressing room.

❦ 5 ❦

HUNTER

R age blurred my vision. My claws extended and dug into the underside of the wood table.

Javier just sealed his fate. I'd slay him as painfully as possible, feasting on his entrails while he begged for mercy.

Venom dripped from my fangs as I battled the overpowering urge to charge across the strip club and attack.

The only thing keeping me in my seat was the fucking chip in my head and the knowledge that my dancer had escaped Javier's attempts at mind control.

Although Alpha shifters possessed the ability to compel humans and weaker shifters, only the most craven would use it to seduce a female.

I gnashed my teeth together, wishing I was grinding Javier's bones to dust.

After compelling the club owner to bring Lee to see him, Javier had made her an offer most wouldn't refuse.

I was proud of my dancer for not taking the bait. From my weeks of stalking her, I knew she was hard up for cash.

Javier, on the other hand, had loads of money. Drugs,

human trafficking, and extortion had made him obscenely wealthy. But when dollar bills didn't get him what he wanted, he resorted to the same tactics he'd used to take over the Latin American cartels—mind control and intimidation.

Lee hadn't stood a chance.

The moment the fucker compelled her to want sex, she'd grown wet for him. I could still smell the sweet scent of her arousal from across the club.

If Javier hadn't been interrupted, he might have compelled her to mate with him right then and there.

Not that I would have allowed that to happen.

Orders or no orders, she'd have sex with Javier over my dead and broken body.

She's mine.

Now that I'd scented the perfume of her lust, my craving for her bordered on pain. Shaking with need, I tracked Lee's power walk from Javier's booth toward the curtains that led to the bathrooms and VIP rooms.

The sound of wood splintering had me looking down at the table. My claws had ripped straight through the top of it. *I'm losing control.*

I tensed, waiting for my handler to notice the spike in my arousal and blast me with a punishing electric shock. When nothing happened, I slowly let out a deep breath. *Jen must not be monitoring me closely.* Which meant...

A slow grin spread across my face. I retracted my claws and glanced around the club.

The old man in the cowboy hat had left. A blonde dancer bounced around the stage to an annoying as fuck pop song. Donna and her club owner husband were staring at the television over the bar. Javier was discussing another shipment of weapons with his enforcers. And the dominatrix was offering the jackass at the table in front of me a private dance.

No one was watching me.

This is my chance.

I'd darted halfway across the club before I noticed Donna turning to look in my direction.

"Wow, you're moving fast, Sly," she exclaimed loudly.

Two of Javier's enforcers turned to look at me.

Fuck. "Y-yeah." Remembering my act, I stopped and swayed in place. "Need to piss."

Donna let out a grating laugh.

The enforcers turned their attention back to Javier.

I'd almost blown my cover. Cursing my recklessness, I stumbled through the dark velvet curtain. Despite the dim lighting, I had no problem making out the bathroom door to my left and a row of VIP rooms that led down the hallway. Across from the rooms was a set of stairs my dancer was climbing.

With my speed and reflexes, I could have rushed up the stairs and snatched her. But I didn't want to risk her screams attracting unwanted attention.

"Wait," I called out, my booming voice carrying over the pop music.

The dark-haired beauty stopped mid-step, gifting me with the incredible view of her muscular calves and firm ass before she spun around. "Sly?"

The body glitter dusting her naked torso momentarily distracted me. It glistened, making her look wet and delicious. I flared my nostrils and drank her scent in—musky vanilla with darker undercurrents of desire.

My cock throbbed and the sharp barbs along its length snagged the fabric of my pants.

"Sly," she said again, coming down a step. "Are you okay?"

With a start, I realized she was calling me by my alias. "Yes." My voice sounded like broken glass. I cleared my throat. "You dropped something."

"I did?" she came down another step.

I retrieved the feather from my pocket and held it out to her. "I found this on the floor."

"Oh, that. You can keep it," she said with a dismissive wave.

I willed her to take it. "Can't you glue it back on?"

She sighed. "Sure. Thanks."

I held my breath as she took the last step down and reached for the feather.

Her golden skin pressed against mine, and a frisson of electricity passed between us.

I inhaled sharply, savoring the contact. A loud purr-like growl rumbled through my chest.

Lee started at the inhuman sound.

Fuck. Moving in a blur, I dropped the feather, snapped my hand around hers, and twisted her around so her back was against my chest. Then, I clamped my other hand over her mouth and carried her into the closest room.

She let out muffled shrieks, trying to punch me with her free hand.

"Calm down." I tightened my arm around her, pinning her hands to her side. Then I yanked the red velvet curtains closed behind us.

Agonizing pain pulsed through my head. I'd blown my cover, violating one of my handler's orders. My chip would punish me until I rectified the situation. As the painful shocks intensified, I continued shifting into my natural form.

My dancer had to sense my shoulders broadening and my muscles thickening around her. Still, she fought me. She knocked off my sunglasses and buried her teeth into the flesh of my palm.

The mounting pain summoned my beast. A deep roar thundered from my lips as my muscles contorted and my bones snapped.

Her struggles became more frantic.

My beast relished in her terror, wanting to assert its dominance. As I continued shifting, the top of my aching head collided with the small chandelier hanging above us. The tinkling of the chandelier crystals brought me to my senses.

No!

Taking deep ragged breaths, I stopped the transformation.

My beast thrashed just below the surface. It urged me to wrap my jaws around the smooth column of her throat and press my fangs against her fluttering pulse until she submitted to me.

Unaware her struggles were putting her in mortal danger, my dancer lifted one of her stilettos and tried to kick me with the pointed end.

I easily evaded the sharp heel. "The more you fight, the more I crave you." Trying to ignore the mounting pain in my head, I rubbed my hard cock against her back.

She went still. Her wildly beating heart sounded in my ear.

Not wanting to injure her, I adjusted my hold and her bare nipples grazed the top of my arm. A shudder rocked through me. I'd been waiting weeks to touch her like this.

Take her, my beast urged.

My breath sawed in and out. *No!* I would not hurt her.

Summoning the frayed edges of my self-control, I flung her away and forced myself to regain a more human shape.

She stumbled into the small raised platform in the middle of the room. Using her arms to push herself up, she opened her mouth to scream.

Fuck. I hated resorting to mind control, but she and the chip in my head left me no choice. "Look at my eyes."

"Th-they're glowing," she cried. "What are you?"

Infusing power into my words, I said, "You're under my control."

Her expression went blank. "I'm under your control," she recited back.

"Relax. I mean you no harm. We're good friends and you're happy to see me."

"We're good friends," she repeated in a dazed voice.

"Friends with benefits," the asshole in me couldn't resist adding.

Her eyes glazed over, the tension left her body, and her arms fell to her side.

All at once, the pain in my head disappeared. She'd believe whatever I wanted her to believe. She'd do whatever I wanted her to do. I motioned at the armless black couch behind the platform. "Please, sit."

She obediently walked over to the couch and sat on the shiny cushions that smelled of things I didn't want to think about. Then, she looked at me expectantly.

I hated myself in that moment. Lee was made of steel. She didn't let anyone tell her what to do, including her shyster landlord or her too handsy boss at Hooters. And I'd taken that from her.

Guilt punched me in the gut. I was no better than Javier preying on her.

But what delicious prey she is.

I couldn't help but stare at her sparkling nipples.

All I had to do was utter the words, and she'd offer them to me. After I'd licked and sucked them, I'd bury my face in her pussy.

My beast purred in anticipation of tasting her. I'd make her orgasm over and over until she begged me to claim her.

Seeming to pick up on my lust, Lee licked her lips.

I groaned. Every cell in my body clamored for me to take her. I reached for her arm. Almost too late, I saw that my claws were fully extended. I quickly jammed my hand into my pocket, only to shred a hole straight through the fabric.

Better the jacket than her skin. Fuck. I can't touch her.

The realization flayed me. She was human, or at least as vulnerable as one.

I was nearly twice her size in my natural form. If I shifted into my beast as I often did when I lost control, our proportions would be even more ridiculous. How could she handle razor-sharp claws, poisonous fangs, and a monstrous barbed cock?

She can't. She'll end up like the others.

A howl of desperation caught in the back of my throat. *What kind of sick irony is this?* I'd found my mate but couldn't claim her.

"You're so tall," Lee said in a breathless voice. "Are you a baller?" Without waiting for me to respond, she answered her own question. "No. You're way too muscular. Are you a body-builder?"

I shook my head.

She studied me. "Your hair is incredible. Do you get highlights?"

I shook my head, not knowing what highlights even were.

She angled her head to the side to stare at my face. "I've never seen metallic gold eyes like yours before either. Are they contacts?"

"No." I retrieved my sunglasses and put them back on. Her inspection of me was making me feel self-conscious.

"Even with your sharp teeth, you're gorgeous," she said in a husky voice. The scent of her sweet musk grew stronger.

She finds me attractive? It shouldn't have mattered, but for some reason it did.

She patted the cushion next to her. "Come here. I want to explore those benefits between us."

Disbelief locked me in place. Even at the club, I'd never seen my dancer proposition any male this way. *But now she wants me?* It made no sense.

In a flash of clarity, I realized what was really happening. *She's still under Javier's compulsion.* In priming her to want him, he'd left her receptive to anyone. *Even a beast like me.*

I wouldn't take advantage of her and I sure as shit wouldn't allow him or anyone else to either.

Pushing a heavy amount of compulsion into my words, I said, "Ignore what Javier told you. You don't need to be touched."

"But I do..." she said in a breathless voice. She rubbed her hand slowly up her thigh. "Will you touch me?"

Alarm bells went off in my head. My compulsion never failed, except for the one time I tried to use it on a handler. I hadn't known then that he and the other Titan soldiers were immune to mind control. My mistake had nearly cost me my life.

I tried again, infusing power into every word. "You're not attracted to Javier."

She blinked. "But I am attracted to him. He's so handsome. And his eyes... He has beautiful eyes like yours."

My confusion gave way to a stunning realization—I couldn't undo Javier's compulsion. And that meant...

Javier is more powerful than me.

Impossible! I was the deadliest and most powerful shifter alive.

As my dancer crooked her finger at me, I finally understood why I'd been ordered not to engage Javier.

The military didn't want to risk me falling under his control.

But Jen could have at least warned me. Unless... this was some kind of test. A fucking diabolical test that pit my mating instincts against my programming.

Of course.

They wanted to know if I would follow orders or go after my mate. They'd even given me the impression that I was unmonitored. I snorted under my breath. I should have known better.

The military would never allow me that kind of freedom.

There was probably an entire team of handlers standing by to haul me away the minute I went AWOL. No doubt I'd join my fallen siblings in their unmarked grave if I failed this test.

A trickle of sweat streamed down my face. *Well, I'll show them.* I'd follow their damn orders. I'd get the intel and return to base. Later, when shit hit the fan, I'd find a way to escape and save my mate. *Opportunity comes from chaos, right?*

My dancer reached out for me. "Sit with me. Touch me."

The murmur of voices from the room next door saved me from insanity. "I can't, dirty dancer. Get your stuff and leave this place." From weeks of stalking her, I knew the old man would take her straight home. She couldn't get into too much trouble there.

"Stay at your house until I come for you."

"You'll see me later?"

No one had ever looked at me with such longing. My chest grew tight, and I fought the urge to drag her into my arms. "Yes. Now close your eyes and forget everything that happened since you left Javier. You can open your eyes in one minute."

"Okay."

As she closed her eyes, I did the hardest thing I'd ever done in my life—I walked away from the female I now knew was my mate.

✤ 6 ✤

LEE

I came to my senses, startled to find myself in one of the VIP rooms. More than a little freaked out, I glanced around the empty walk-in closet-sized space.

What happened? The last thing I remembered was walking away from Javier as fast as I could.

Why make a pit stop here? And why sit on one of the nasty couches even the cleaning crew didn't dare touch? Ew!

As I peeled myself off the sticky vinyl, the unmistakable sound of leather smacking skin made me jump.

Havana must be working the professor extra hard in the next room.

I was glad it was her and not me pretending to enjoy his company. But, for some strange reason, the moaning from the other room made my stomach tighten.

Maybe I'm missing out on something... something big. Maybe Javier is right. Maybe I want to be touched.

My skin warmed at the thought of the drug lord's hands on my body. My breathing shallowed as I imagined accepting his offer. *Maybe I should go to him right now.*

Smack.

"You're such a naughty boy," Havana said in the room next door.

I blinked. *What the hell is wrong with me?* I needed to find Uncle Duncan. He'd been waiting long enough.

Ducking through the red velvet curtain, I rushed up the side stairs and headed to the dressing room. It was empty.

Not having to see Jess was about the only good thing to happen to me today. I let out the tense breath I'd been holding and walked over to the lockers. Mine was next to Cami's. As usual, she hadn't bothered to shut hers and her lingerie spilled out onto the floor.

Shaking my head, I picked up the hot pink teddy and shoved it back inside her locker.

Then I opened my locker and threw on a thick cable-knit sweater and worn jeans. My aching feet practically moaned in approval as I slipped into socks and my old boots. Each layer of clothing gave me more confidence and forced away that weird tingling in my stomach.

I won't take Javier's offer. I'm not for sale.

I looked down at the hundred-dollar bills in my hand.

Well. Not all of me, anyway.

I carefully folded the bills and put them in my purse along with the singles still sitting on my vanity counter. The invisible weight I'd been carrying lessened. I had enough money to bail Eden out of jail and maybe enough left over for a nice meal to celebrate Reed's birthday.

Not too shabby.

Once I'd gathered my things, I stood in the dressing room doorway chewing my lip in indecision.

Do I go home or talk to Max? I wanted to confront my boss about the impossible position he'd put me in with Javier, but, at the same time, I didn't want to keep Uncle Duncan waiting even longer.

My head throbbed to the beat of Cami's sugar pop music.

Home. Definitely home.

I really didn't have another stressful meeting in me. Not after working a double shift at the restaurant and dancing two sets.

I'll rip Max a new one tomorrow.

Decision made, I left the dressing room just as one of the new girls was walking in. Giving a tired wave to the green-haired woman, I headed to the door behind the stage. I normally avoided the back exit since it led to an alley, but tonight I wanted to avoid another potential run in with Javier.

I almost changed my mind when I opened the door and a freezing blast of urine-scented air hit my face. *Ugh. Why can't people use bathrooms?*

Moving into the alley, I rubbed my arms to ward off the chill.

Damn Eden for stealing my jacket. That was the last straw. I'd finally had enough of her shenanigans. *When I bail her out, I'm reading her the riot act. She'll forget about all this bleeding-heart animal rights crap and get a real job or... or I'll throw her out of the house.*

I straightened my spine in resolve.

An inner voice whispered, *It's your job to protect her.* I shook my head, trying to shake loose the words that had haunted me most of my life.

Eden is an adult now. She needs to act like it. I've been carrying her long enough.

For a moment, I fantasized about how different my life might've been if Gran hadn't died.

I wouldn't have had to assume guardianship of Eden and Reed. I would've finished high school and joined my best friends in the Peace Corps. Right now, I'd be traveling the world and Saguaro Valley, Arizona would be nothing more than a fading image in the rearview mirror of my life.

The sound of loud chewing pierced my melancholy. My first thought was some stray dogs had gotten into the dumpster. But all the dogs in town had been euthanized months ago. Confused, I peered down the alley.

The dim, flickering light from the parking lot illuminated the shape of a large man hunched over something.

What's he doing?

I took two steps closer. As my eyes adjusted, I saw a pair of platform heels sticking out from underneath the man.

Oh, my God. He's attacking a woman.

Adrenaline flooded my veins.

I have to get help.

I backtracked to the club door. I jerked the handle, remembering too late it automatically locked to the outside. "Help, someone's being attacked." I beat on the door, hoping someone would hear me.

The man lurched to his feet.

Crap. My heart raced as I fumbled around in my purse for pepper spray. For the first time, I was grateful to my uncle for insisting I carry it. I held the canister outstretched in front of me. "Stay where you are. I've called the police. They're on their way." I prayed he couldn't hear the lie in my shaky voice.

The man stumbled toward me, making a strange clicking sound with his teeth. His head was canted so far to the right it looked as if he was about to topple over.

What the hell is wrong with him? "Stay back."

Ignoring me, he lumbered into the light. The man looked to be in his early twenties. His cloudy, unfocused gaze creeped me out even more than the bright red blood coating his face and shirt.

My heart hammered against my sternum. *What happened to him, and what did he do to that woman?*

The woman in question lurched upright. Her long, bright red hair extensions were unmistakable.

"Jess, are you oka—" My words cut off as she stumbled into the light.

Her yellow minidress was shredded down the front. Even worse, her intestines streamed out of an open wound in her stomach like grizzly Christmas garland.

Oh, God. "Jess..."

She lifted her head and met my gaze with eerie white eyes. Then she gnashed her teeth together and tottered in my direction.

For a moment, every muscle in my body froze. The pepper spray bottle dropped from my trembling hand and hit the pavement with a thunk.

This can't be happening.

The man staggered closer. The horrible sound of his teeth clicking echoed in my ears.

Coming to my senses, I turned and ran through the alley. I made it to the parking lot and frantically scanned for Uncle Duncan's beat-up truck. It was gone. Other than a few parked vehicles, the lot was deserted.

Oh, crap. I'd taken too long. He'd left me.

A whimper escaped my lips.

Light blazed from the windows of the sex shop like a homing beacon. I rushed through the door. Bells jangled as I slammed it behind me.

A fiftyish man with a thick paunch glanced at me through the rows of multicolored dildos lined up across the counter. "Good evening. What can I—"

With my chest heaving, I panted, "Zombie."

The man, who's thinning red hair and lime-green bowling shirt made him look like an over-the-hill leprechaun, shook his head. "Sorry, no zombies. But we have an entire section dedicated to vampire role-play. It's over by the lubes." He motioned to the left of the store.

"There are zombies outside." I knew I sounded crazy. I half expected him to throw me out of his store.

Instead, the man nodded. "I knew it was just a matter of time." He leaned down and grabbed a shotgun from behind the counter. "It's closing time." He marched to the door and flipped the sign hanging on the handle from Open to Closed. "My name is Cal."

"I'm Lee."

"This is only the beginning, Lee. I've been watching the news. Things are going to get bad. Real bad. I give it forty-eight hours before they overrun the city."

I swallowed hard. "Shouldn't we call the police?"

His laugh sounded like a wheeze. "They can't help us. Our only chance is to gather weapons and supplies and wait the worst of it out. I have a well-stocked underground shelter." He gave me a head-to-toe scan and licked his lips. "You're welcome to join me."

My skin crawled and my internal creeper alarm flashed red. "Um, thanks, but I need to get home."

He frowned. "Suit yourself. Can I give you a lift?"

Hmm. Creepy sex shop owner vs. zombies. Damn. This is a no-win situation.

Taking my silence as a refusal, he shook his head. "At least let me walk you to the street." He pushed the door open.

"Thanks." I followed him out.

As we walked past the alley, I couldn't help stopping and peering through the darkness.

It looked empty.

Did I imagine it?

I rubbed my eyes. *Maybe I did.* I'd been working a lot lately. And, if I was being honest, I couldn't remember the last time I'd gotten over four hours of sleep.

Cal darted ahead, stopping every few feet to survey the

handful of vehicles occupying the unpaved parking lot his store shared with Eros.

Country music filtered out of the strip club. I stopped in my tracks. Jess used that song in her routine...

How can she be inside dancing when I'd just seen her—

The realization of what had really happened slammed into me like a cement truck.

Goddamn it. There were no walking dead. There was just a bitchy stripper with a chip on her shoulder and a love for cruel practical jokes. I should've known better. It was just like the time she'd put talcum powder in my hair dryer or the time she'd glued all my makeup to the counter. She'd laughed and told everyone in the club how she punked me.

Jess was a genius with stage makeup. It wouldn't have taken much to do a convincing zombie look. White contacts, fake blood, and leftover Halloween props...

I kicked at the gravel, wishing it was her head. Of all the nights for her to test me... if I wasn't so damned tired, I'd stalk into the club and slap the smug expression off her face.

"Shh," Cal hissed at me as he darted around vehicles like some kind of wannabe SWAT officer.

The ridiculousness of the whole thing caught up to me. I let out a strained laugh. "Thank you, Cal. I've got it from here."

"But... the zombies."

"Someone was just playing a joke on me. I appreciate your help though. You'd better put the gun away. There are some pretty bad dudes in the club who might think you're looking for trouble." I nodded at several black Mercedes that belonged to Javier and his goons.

Cal's eyes widened. "The threat is real. You need to prepare yourself for the apocalypse."

Okayyy. This conversation just took a left turn into crazy town. "I'll see you later."

Cal grabbed for my arm. "You'll die if you go out alone and unarmed."

He's insane. Heart in my throat, I backed away.

Cal followed me, tightening his grip on his shotgun. "You need to come with me now."

7

REED

"Come on, Reed," Aubry urged, her huge breasts hanging in my face. Some kind of magic must've kept them from busting out of their confinement, because neither the tight corset she wore nor the laws of gravity were on their side.

Forcing my gaze from the outline of her pale pink nipples to her model-beautiful face, I shook my head. "Sorry, not tonight." *Or any other night.*

"Don't you want to...?" She trailed off, looking confused.

I'd bet the stack of twenties in my pocket that my refusal was a first for her. Most guys would probably jump at the chance to get in her pants.

But I wasn't like most guys. And there was only one pair of pants I wanted to get into. *Lee's.*

Still, I didn't want to be rude. Trying to soften the rejection, I said, "Thanks for keeping me company and for inspiring that killer line in my song."

Aubry blinked. "You realize I'm offering to rock your world right now."

"Yeah, but I'm going to have to pass. My friend Dexter

would love to talk to you." I jabbed my finger in direction of the crowded kitchen.

Aubry frowned. "Is it because I bit you? If you're not into that, that's okay. I can do vanilla too." She suddenly looked younger and more vulnerable.

"It's not you, it's me." *Or rather, it's an even more beautiful brunette that stole my heart years ago.*

"That's what my ex said too." Her eyes took on a glassy sheen.

Ah, Jesus. I hated when they cried. *Why does this keep happening to me?* Ronnie and Dexter spent every waking minute hitting on girls, while I purposefully kept my distance. But it was always me they came after. It made no sense.

"It's cool. I get it." Her lower lip quivered, and I could tell she was close to losing it.

"Panorama plays in five," Ronnie shouted from the hallway.

A loud cheer went up among the partygoers, and they began spilling into the living room.

Aubry let out a muffled sob.

Morgan and Sam looked up from their instruments to stare at her.

"What's her damage?" a woman in a pink tank top said loudly from the lap of the guy sitting in Gran's old recliner.

Deciding Aubry didn't need an audience, I stood. All at once the jungle juice hit me and I had to fight back a wave of vertigo. I took a deep breath and the dizzy feeling went away. Making a promise to stay away from the stuff, I grabbed her arm. "Come on, I'll show you my room."

Aubry sniffed and let me pull her through the growing crowd of people.

I took her down the hall and opened my door.

Aubry wiped her eyes. "I don't know why I'm so

emotional tonight. It's cool if you aren't into me. You don't need to pity fuck me or anything."

"I wasn't planning on it," I said, waving her inside.

She gave me a shuttered look and walked in. I followed her gaze as it bounced between my unmade bed, the band posters hanging on the walls, and the collection of trophies and medals on my dresser.

"Sorry, about the mess." I kicked aside some magazines and the broken amp I'd been tinkering with. Guess I had no reason to fix it now.

After a moment, she wandered over to my open closet. Inside were a bunch of my shirts and a pegboard where I'd hung my old bats. "You're really into flannel."

I shrugged. "They're comfortable." And, more importantly, they had long sleeves.

She grabbed the cuff of one shirt and waved it at me. "You shouldn't hide your scars. Some women find them sexy."

It was as if she saw straight through me and I didn't know how to respond.

Aubry turned her attention to the pegboard. "You play baseball?"

"Played," I corrected, deciding to close my bedroom door. I didn't want to give Aubry the wrong idea, but it was a relief to shut out the music and loud chatter of the partygoers.

Aubry's pretty green eyes narrowed in challenge. "Were you any good?"

I shrugged, not wanting to brag. I'd been damn good if the full ride scholarship I'd gotten to Arizona State was any sign. But ASU was in Phoenix, and Lee was here in Saguaro Valley. So, I'd passed.

One day Lee was going to kick my ass when she found out.

Aubry plucked a bat off the board and inspected it. "I played softball throughout high school. I was really good."

"What position?" I asked to be polite.

"Pitcher."

"Cool. Why did you stop playing?"

"Damon," she said softly. "I can't believe I gave up my dream of playing in the nationals for that asshole."

"Is that your ex?" I asked, putting two and two together.

She nodded, chewing her lower lip. "We broke up last week on our three-year anniversary."

"That sucks he made you quit baseball." Lee would have never asked me to quit. In fact, she'd worked her schedule around all of my in-town games. It'd both embarrassed and thrilled me to have her screaming my name in the stands.

Aubry's eyes flashed. "Damon didn't make me do anything. I quit to spend more time with him." She put the bat back on the pegboard and sighed. "I should have listened to my mom. She always said, don't sacrifice your future for a good lay."

I laughed. "Your mom sounds like mine." Mom had never minced words.

We shared a smile.

Some of her black lipstick had rubbed off on her front teeth, but I didn't want to make her feel bad, so I didn't mention it.

She sauntered over to my bed and sat down.

The mattress sloshed underneath her.

"Ah!" she cried, jumping back up.

"It's a waterbed," I warned too late.

She giggled. "That's so retro."

"Right? A guy down the street was just throwing it away. I had to save it." Before she could judge me for taking someone's trash, I quickly added, "I cleaned it really well. It's fun to sleep on."

Aubry looked at me through her thick black lashes. "I'll bet it would be fun to do other things on, too." She sat down slowly and motioned me to sit next to her. "Why don't we try it out?"

I rubbed the back of my neck, wishing she wouldn't keep circling her horse around that wagon. "Look, I think you're cool as shit, but I'm into someone else."

"I know," she said, not even pretending she hadn't heard it from Ronnie. "But your someone else can't be very nice if she doesn't reciprocate."

"That's where you are wrong," I said, leaning against my dresser. "Lee's the nicest person I've ever met. She's always thinking about everyone else before herself. And she's smart too. She rocked the SATs and I know she could have gone to a good college if she'd graduated."

Aubry rolled her eyes. "I'll bet she's pretty too."

"Well, they didn't make her the headliner at Eros for nothing."

Aubry's jaw dropped. "She's a stripper?"

A familiar wave of frustration and anger coiled in my chest. "Yeah, but Lee's not like that..." I didn't quite know how to express that Lee was nothing like the other dancers.

Aubry pursed her lips. "I see. And where is this paragon among women?"

As I tried to puzzle out what the word paragon meant, she added, "Where does she live?"

"Here." I glanced at the digital clock on my nightstand. "She should be heading back with our uncle now."

"You two are related? Man, this gets better and better."

I felt my face heat. "It's not like that. Her grandmother took me in after my mother died."

Aubry inhaled sharply. "I'm sorry."

I waved away her apology. "It happened a while ago, but Lee and I have been living together ever since. Her room is right there." I pointed at the wall behind the bed.

"Wow. Okay." Aubry looked stunned.

As she stared at the wall, it occurred to me that I'd just spilled my guts to a virtual stranger. *What if she says something to Lee?*

I cleared my throat. "She doesn't exactly know how I feel, and I'd appreciate it if you kept this conversation on the down low."

Aubry's eyes widened. "Totally. I don't even know her."

"Thanks." I don't know why, but I trusted Aubry.

"I might not be a stripper, but I've got some killer moves if you want to see them." She sloshed up and down on my bed. When I shook my head, she sighed. "Well, I had to try one last time, didn't I?"

"Why?" I had to ask. "I mean, I'm not looking for compliments. I'm just trying to understand why you'd pick me over all the other guys out there that are dying to talk to you?"

"Let's turn that around. Why do you chase after Lee instead of accepting the offer of a sexual goddess?" She gestured down at herself.

I opened my mouth to defend my love, but she held up her hand.

"Conventional psychology would say we both have deep-seated insecurities. Our low self-concept deludes us into chasing the unobtainable, because at our core we think we are unworthy of love."

Well, fuck.

Aubry let out a gusty breath of air. "But I think the reason is even simpler. It's easy to fall for what we can never have. It's scary and hard to love what's possible."

"That's some next level shit right there." I rubbed my beard, thoughtfully. I'd never thought to question my feelings for Lee. *Do I love her because I know she could never love me back?*

"I have my moments." Aubry smiled, and this time there was no coyness to it.

"You're really easy to talk to. That ex of yours really lost out."

Aubry flushed and smoothed out a wrinkle in her skirt. "Thanks for saying that."

I chuckled. "I don't usually go around telling my business to random people."

She shared my laugh. "Well, I'm a psych major so there's that."

"Are you shitting me?"

When she shook her head, I laughed again. "Classic."

She gave me a serious look. "Can I give you some advice though?"

"As long as I don't have to pay for it, Dr. Aubry."

"You should tell her how you feel."

I rubbed my chest, feeling the thick ridges of my scars through the flannel. "Yeah. Someday." But not today. *Definitely not today.*

Aubrey pressed her black lips together. "Someday isn't guaranteed. Today might be all you have."

I tried to lighten the mood. "Now you sound like a true therapist."

Tears gathered in her eyes.

Crap. "I'm guessing you speak from experience."

She nodded. "I lost my mom back in April. Canine flu."

It was my turn to say, "I'm sorry."

She sighed. "Mom hated Damon. She didn't like that he was kind of married."

"Kind of married?"

She gave me a sheepish look. "I know. It sounds bad, but it's a long story. Anyway, Mom and I had a bad fight about him. I knew we'd eventually make up. We always did. But I kept putting off calling her..." Her voice grew tight. "I never got the chance to tell her she was right, and that I loved her."

"I'm sure she knew."

Aubry sniffed and wiped her eyes. "Don't be like me. Don't wait for someday."

"Okay. Can I give you some advice too?"

She tilted her head to the side, "Sure."

"Give my friend Dexter a chance. He's a good guy."

She laughed. "Why not? You said he was in the kitchen?"

"Yup."

The bed undulated beneath her as she pushed herself up. "Damn, this would be fun to screw on. Are you sure you won't reconsider?"

I shook my head, apologetically.

"Your loss." She sashayed over to the door and opened it. Before stepping out, she whirled around. "Just so you know, I would have totally rocked your world."

"I know you would have."

Flashing me another smile, she left.

For a fleeting moment, I wanted to run after her and drag her back into my room.

Aubry wasn't turned off by my scars, and she seemed to get me in a way most people didn't. Furthermore, unlike Lee, she wanted to bone me.

And what did I do? I sent her right into the arms of my friend.

I'm such an idiot. Groaning, I strode to the door and rejoined the party I already wished was over.

8

LEE

"Is there a problem?" a familiar gravelly voice said behind me.

I spun around. The sight of Uncle Duncan grimacing at the sex shop owner had me releasing a tense breath. "I thought you'd left."

My uncle gave me an apologetic look. "Sorry, I was just picking up some smokes. Is this guy botherin' you?" His hand rested on the holstered revolver he always carried.

Cal's gaze darted from me to Uncle Duncan. He shifted his grip on the shotgun as if nervous the silver-haired, mustached cowboy would start shooting.

"Cal was just making sure I made it to the street safely." I turned to the bug-eyed sex shop owner. "Thanks for your help."

Cal nodded. "I'll check out the alley for you."

"Don't worry about it." I knew all he'd find there was some fake blood.

I so owe Jess for this.

"Better safe than sorry," Cal said, marching into the alley.

Uncle Duncan shook his head. "Interestin' friends you

have." He offered me his arm, and I let him escort me across the street. The familiar smell of stale cigarette smoke clinging to his fringed leather jacket calmed me with every breath I took.

As we walked to the liquor store, I noticed his limp was more pronounced than usual. I started to ask if his prosthetic was hurting. Thankfully, I caught myself in time. My uncle was sensitive about his lost limb.

When we were kids, he'd told Eden, Reed, and me he'd lost his left leg in a grizzly bear attack. After a while, his story changed to include a ferocious shark, and then later his leg became the casualty of a light saber battle. It wasn't until I was older that I'd learned he'd lost it in the Vietnam War. Thankfully, an unknown soldier had shoved my uncle off a land mine before he'd lost more than a limb.

A car filled with rowdy college-age men nearly ran us over as it peeled into the liquor store parking lot.

Uncle Duncan and I gave them matching one-finger salutes. The all-too-familiar interaction relaxed me further.

It was just an average Thursday night. Sure, half the bars and clubs on Fourth Avenue were boarded up, casualties of the economic effects of the canine flu. But the sky was alive with helicopters flying to the nearby army base, and people were cheering inside the pool hall down the street.

When we reached the liquor store parking lot, Uncle Duncan moved ahead of me to open the passenger door of his rusted-out white truck.

Wanting to get home and forget about my hellish evening, I eagerly jumped in. The inside of the truck carried the lingering scent of wet dog. With a pang of sadness, I glanced into the backseat and saw Buddy's plaid blanket still laid out for him. The old black lab had been Uncle Duncan's trusty companion for years. It was heartbreaking that he'd had to be put down like all the other dogs.

My uncle walked around the front of the truck and eased into the driver's seat.

I bit my lip, stifling the offer to drive. The last time I'd suggested it, the old man had chewed me out, insisting he'd been driving with his peg leg longer than I'd been alive.

As Uncle Duncan pulled out of the parking lot, he cast me a reprimanding look from under the brim of his hat. "I wish you'd quit strippin'. You're too smart for that kinda thing."

I stiffened, readying myself for the lecture that was sure to come. "We need the income."

"I've done told you a thousand times, I'll help you kids out."

I shook my head, thinking of the paltry sum of VA disability money he received a month. It was barely enough to cover his lot at the trailer park. "Keep your money. We'll get by."

"Goddamn it. You Walker women are so stubborn. Your Gran was the same way and your mother..." His voice trailed off.

We never talked about my mother. Ever.

I clutched my purse to my chest, wishing I could remember more about her. Time had eroded my memories of her face and the sound of her voice.

Uncle Duncan continued driving in pensive silence. Soon bars and clubs gave way to run-down apartment complexes and college housing. The next turn brought us to my neighborhood.

The sight of weed-filled yards and old cars up on cinder blocks was depressing. One day we'd earn enough money to move somewhere nicer. Until that day, I'd just have to grit my teeth and—

The sound of blaring music jolted me. My single-story rental was still two houses away, but there was no missing the throngs of people congregated in the front yard.

I took a deep breath. *It's Reed's birthday*, I reminded myself.

A cluster of people I didn't recognize lounged on the worn saggy couch under the carport. They chatted and gulped liquid from red cups. My mood darkened further. *There better not be a keg.*

Uncle Duncan parked the truck in front of the house. "Looks like you've got some company."

I gritted my teeth in frustration. "It's Reed's birthday."

Although he may not live to see another one if the cops show up.

"Oh yeah." Uncle Duncan reached under the center console and cursed. "Dammit, I forgot to bring Reed's gift with me."

Of course, he got Reed a gift, because that's what you did for family on their birthdays.

I slunk down in my seat, feeling even more like a jerk for forgetting. "We're going to celebrate tomorrow. Come to dinner with us and give him your gift then."

My uncle shook his head. "I can't. I'm driving up to the Rim to check on the cabin. Ricky's gonna pick you up at the club and drive you home tomorrow."

"Ricky? Are you two seeing each other again?" I smiled thinking of the foulmouthed, heavily bearded manager of Duncan's trailer park.

My uncle flushed. Ignoring my question, he snapped his fingers. "Hey, why don't you kids come up to the cabin with me? We can hike and fish. Like old times."

Fond memories of summers spent visiting his run-down cabin flashed in my mind. "That sounds amazing."

He gave me a jack-o'-lantern grin, revealing a handful of missing teeth. "Great, then I'll swing by and pick y'all up tomorrow morning."

All too quickly, I remembered my two shifts at the restaurant and my set at the club. I shook my head sadly. "I wish I could. I have to work."

His smile faded. "Well, think about it. I'll still come by around nine with Reed's present. If you change your mind, we can all head out."

"Sounds good." I slid across the cab to plant a quick kiss on his cheek. "Thanks for the ride and coming to the club."

"It's the least I can do," he said as I jumped out of the truck.

I gave him a quick wave and turned to march through the yard. There were at least a dozen crumpled red cups lying like grave markers in the dead grass. Refusing to give into my anger, I took a deep breath and navigated around them.

Reed will pick this up first thing tomorrow.

I pushed past the people loitering on the front step. A few familiar faces called out, "Hey, Lee." Not in the mood for small talk, I ignored them and stepped through the open door.

The smell of weed and the sound of loud music assaulted my senses. I clamped my hands over my ears and tried to peer past the wall-to-wall people. The living room had been overtaken by music equipment and Reed's band.

Ronnie, shirtless and wearing too-tight skinny jeans, crooned unintelligible lyrics into a microphone, while Sam flexed his enormous biceps banging away on his drum set. Morgan's black hair obscured his pockmarked face as he strummed his guitar and Reed... Reed stood by the speakers smoking a clove in jeans and a blue flannel shirt.

Why isn't Reed playing?

With one last wail, Ronnie finished the god-awful song. The crowd must've been drunk because they hooted and howled their appreciation. Always theatrical, Ronnie bowed several times. "Thank you. Thank you. That song was dedicated to our former bandmate who is celebrating his twentieth birthday tonight. Reed, we're gonna miss you, man."

Former bandmate?

I blinked in confusion. The band was everything to Reed. Just last week he'd been trying to convince me they were close to signing with a record label. I'd laughed and told him to wake up and smell reality. His band had as much chance of making it big as I had in making it to the Peace Corps now. Some dreams had to die bitter deaths. But I didn't intend on Reed doing something as drastic as quitting.

A heavy wave of guilt blindsided me.

As if sensing me, Reed looked up. All at once I was snared by his electric-blue eyes. They contrasted so vividly against his darkly tanned skin they gave him an almost otherworldly appearance. The combo of those eyes with his high cheekbones and long sandy-blond hair made him panty-dropping gorgeous.

That fact wasn't lost on the female partygoers standing around him. I kind of wanted to slap the flirtatious looks off their faces.

Seeming oblivious to their interest, Reed straightened to his lanky six-foot height and pushed away from the huge speaker he'd been leaning against.

Motioning him toward the kitchen, I maneuvered between the wall-to-wall crowd.

Some tall, muscular guy crashed into me, spilling his drink.

Goddamn it. I stared at the beer dripping down the front of my sweater, daring the night to get any worse.

"What a waste of good beer," the guy mumbled.

I gave him a scathing look. Based on his Southern Arizona University sweatshirt and short blond crew cut, he didn't run with Reed's crowd.

Getting his first look at me, the guy's hazel eyes widened,

and a dazed look crossed his face. "Um, I'm... I'm so sorry for spilling my drink." He tried to mop up the wet spot on my chest.

"Get your hands off me." I pushed him away.

"Sorry. Uh. Let me make it up to you. Can I get you a drink?"

"No, thanks."

Seemingly oblivious to my annoyance, he stuck his hand out. "Name's Noah, but everyone calls me Scooter."

"Great. You can scooter out of my way."

He laughed too loud at my lame joke and dropped his hand. "A beautiful woman with a sense of humor. That's a rare thing. Do you live around here?"

I craned my neck to look around his bulging bicep. "You could say that."

"Do you go to SAU?"

Reed appeared next to me and said, "She's out of your league, man." Then tugged me into the kitchen.

"That was a little cold-blooded." Reed was usually nice to a fault. He'd even offered a glass of water to the guy who repossessed our car last month.

"I didn't like the way he was looking at you."

I snorted. "Better not come to the club then." The men there made the drunk college boy look like a gentleman.

Reed's eyes darkened. "I hate that you have to work there."

I opened my mouth to remind him we needed the money but was distracted by the state of the kitchen. The avocado-colored laminate counters were covered in red cups, wadded up chip bags, and bongs. Spying the keg sitting over by the fridge, my skin grew hot and tight. "Reed—"

"Before you say anything, I promise everyone will be out of here by two. Ronnie's going to take the keg with him, and I'll clean the entire house."

A couple of the guys playing beer pong on Gran's old oak dining table waved at Reed. "Awesome party, man. When is the stripper getting here? Ronnie said there would be a stripper."

I stared hard at the peeling white cabinets, pressing my lips together. I couldn't handle this right now. Every part of my life was in crisis. Neither job I had was paying enough to cover our bills. My boss was pimping me out to a drug lord who'd probably end up killing me. My sister was in jail. My house was a disaster and filled to the brim with drunk assholes.

"I have something for you." Reed reached into his jean pocket and pulled out a wad of twenty-dollar bills.

I looked at the cash he pressed into my hand in confusion. "Where did you get this?"

"I sold the bass."

"But you loved that bass." Reed's mom had given it to him for his fourteenth birthday. Just days before the car accident that had taken her life and nearly taken Reed's.

"I need to help you out with the rent, and the time I've been practicing with the band could be better spent looking for a job. I've got more interviews lined up next week. One of those will work out. I know it."

This was too much. Yes, we needed the money. But not at the cost of his dreams. I pushed the bills back at him. "Reed Jarin Marshall, you buy that bass back."

"The big sister act doesn't work with me." He smiled and touched my cheek. His gaze shimmered with an emotion that startled me.

He wasn't blood, but after the accident when Gran took him in, I'd treated him like family. I'd even temporarily made him my ward when Gran died to keep him out of the system. That had only reinforced our familial relationship in my mind. But the way he was looking at me was far from brotherly. My skin tingled under the warmth of his fingers.

Needing some distance, I took a step back. Shoving the cash in my purse, I said, "Fine, I'll keep this for now, but as soon as we have enough money, I'm buying you an even better bass."

"Okay," he said, with a smile that didn't quite reach his eyes. "Here, have a drink." He snagged a red cup off the table, filled it with beer, and handed it to me.

Why the hell not?

I took a sip and choked on the bitter, malty taste. The next sip wasn't too bad. I lifted the cup and tilted it toward Reed. "Happy birthday, bro."

A muscle ticked in his jaw. "I'm not your brother."

"But you're family. You, Uncle Duncan, and Eden."

"True that."

The cheers of the assholes sitting around the table broke the sudden awkwardness between us.

"I'm going to change." I motioned down to the wet stains on my sweater. Without waiting for him to respond, I set the cup of beer down on the counter and headed to my room. I didn't expect to find two half-dressed strangers rolling around on my bed.

The fury I'd been trying to bottle in for the past thirty minutes exploded.

I flipped on the light. "What are you doing?"

Reed's friend Dexter and some dark-haired chick I didn't know, pulled apart.

"Get out!" I screamed.

The woman hastily pulled down her tiny skirt while Dexter gave me an apologetic look. "Sorry, Lee we were just—"

"Trespassing. That's what you were doing. Get the fuck out!"

The chick laughed. "And Reed said you were nice."

I held up my fists. "I'll give you fucking nice, right up your ass."

With almost comical haste, they ran from my room.

I slammed the door behind me and locked it. Crinkling my nose in disgust, I surveyed my wrinkled mink-brown suede comforter.

What would possess people to sneak into a stranger's room?

Still shaking my head, I walked over to my closet. Kneeling on the warped wood floor, I felt for the loose floorboard underneath a stack of shoe boxes. The plank came away in my hands. I reached down into the space and pulled out the money I'd socked away. I added tonight's earnings along with Reed's contribution.

It was enough to cover this month's overdue rent. But we'd also have Eden's latest legal fees to contend with...

With a heavy sigh, I slipped the money back into the hole. As I reassured myself that Gran's small jewelry pouch remained untouched, my fingers brushed against cool metal. Unable to stop myself, I pulled out a two-foot long military knife.

My warped image reflected back at me from the shiny blade. The screams of my mother and sister seemed to reverberate in the air around the deadly weapon. Seeing the knife brought back the horror of that night. Of what my father had done. Of what he'd forced me to do...

Tears burned my eyes as I fell into the darkest of my memories.

❦　9　❦

HUNTER

I forced myself to stay slumped over the cocktail table as my thoughts and emotions spun out in a million directions.

I have a mate.

Years ago, my twin had claimed I'd one day find our female—the mate we were destined for. Ghost said it'd be undeniable, like a lightning strike to my very soul. I'd written his prophesy off as another one of his mad ravings.

Until now.

The visceral reaction I'd had to my dancer could not be denied, and her presence here, at the same club where I'd been assigned, could not be a coincidence. The military must have discovered her existence and then forced me to watch her dance night after night, knowing the effect it would have on me.

My gaze skittered over to where Javier sat with his enforcers. *Had the army arranged for them to come here too?*

It all sounded too far-fetched. I scrubbed a hand over my face, not knowing what to believe. It could be nothing but a crazy coincidence, or it could be another one of their tests.

My life had been filled with their soul-harrowing experiments —each pitting my primal instincts against my military programming. *If it is another test, I can't afford to fail it.*

Not with my mate's life on the line.

A vice clenched tight around my heart as I glanced at the television over the bar. Non-stop images of infected humans attacking the living played across the screen. The shock and horror of the news reporters was reflected in the faces of Donna, Max, and the bartender. They were trying to understand what was happening. But they couldn't. No one could but the army scientists and Dr. Hurran who I suspected had a hand in unleashing this horror on the world.

Dammit. I had to find the bitch. *But how?* Out of the corner of my eye, I watched Javier pointedly ignore the panicked humans watching the news.

He didn't seem the slightest bit concerned or surprised at current world events. *Because the fucker knows what's coming.*

All the boring conversations I'd overheard regarding deliveries of food, equipment, and weapons made sense now. Javier was amassing supplies enough to see him and his faction through the end of days.

Temporarily forgetting my ruse, I sat up straighter in my chair.

And all those construction projects he was overseeing... They had to be fortifications to his compound.

He's been preparing for the apocalypse. And he wants to ride it out with my mate.

I shook my head slightly. No fucking way would I allow that. Frustration ate at me as I tossed back another watered-down drink and looked away from the unfamiliar green-haired female awkwardly thrusting her hips in crotchless chaps on stage. Her terrible dancing and the loud twang of country music blaring through the club made my head throb.

I toyed with the idea of cramming my cocktail napkin into my ears to block out the irritating sound.

That's not all I could block out. A jolt of excitement ran through me. If I couldn't hear Javier's voice, there was no risk of falling under his control and I could happily beat the scientist's location out of him.

My mood sank when I remembered Jen's orders not to approach Javier. The chip in my head made it impossible to ignore a direct order from my handler. However, I'd learned a long time ago that the secret to circumventing my orders was all in my interpretation. The vaguer the order, the more I could misconstrue it and still avoid punishment. Unfortunately, in this case, my orders were pretty clear.

As I tried to think of a workaround, I noticed the dominatrix stalk out of the VIP area and join the other humans at the bar.

Donna looked up at her. "Honey, you need to see this. There's some freaky shit going down."

The dominatrix shook her head. "Tell me about it. I got a guy covered in black veins about to pass out in the VIP room."

My blood ran cold. *The virus is here. Fuck. It's moving fast.* Faster than even the Colonel had predicted.

As the humans continued speaking in panicked tones, two strange males walked into the club. Although the humans didn't notice their arrival, the scent of Lykos was impossible for me to ignore.

Javier's enforcers went on immediate alert and moved in protectively around him.

Keeping my head on the table, I questioned the sanity of wolf shifters who would enter a club filled with feline shifters.

The blond Lykos in the collared shirt and slacks looked confused to be there, but the taller, dark-haired male with the eye patch scanned the place with tactical precision. His one eye skimmed over my hunched form and zeroed in on Javier and his enforcers.

Javier met his gaze and exchanged a tense nod with him.

Interesting. There seemed to be some sort of truce between rival species. In any other circumstances, I might have given more of a shit at that unsettling discovery. But at the moment, all I cared about was getting the intel I needed.

Javier must've said something telepathically to Miguel, one of his enforcers, because the tall, muscular shifter quickly left the club. At the same time, the two Lykos shifters headed back into the VIP area.

I started to tense but reminded myself they were no threat to my dancer. Lee's scent had faded to the point I knew she'd left the club.

Why are the Lykos here?

Maybe Javier had telepathically summoned them to deal with the infected human the dominatrix was worried about. If so, Javier was even more powerful than I'd credited. Not only did he rule his faction and the largest drug cartel in the hemisphere, he wielded incredibly powerful mind control, and was allied with the Lykos.

Suddenly, going up against such an adversary with a few pieces of paper in my ears didn't seem like the brightest idea.

Dammit. I needed a plan and I needed it now. The club owner's next words only added to my mounting frustration.

"We're closing early tonight. Donna, go get Sly up. I'll tell Mr. Diaz and his men that they need to leave." Max looked over at Javier and trembled. "Let's hope they don't kill me..."

I gnashed my teeth together. There went any chance of getting the intel.

Seeming to have overheard the club owner, Javier glanced at his younger brother. "Go start the car while I close out our tab."

Luis, a depraved and blood-thirsty latent who hadn't yet

made his transition into an adult shifter, tossed his long hair behind him. "That's a task for one of the humans. Have Carlos or Nero do it."

Javier leveled his brother with a hard stare. "I. Asked. You."

The other males cringed at the menace in his voice.

Color leeched from Luis's face, but he bared his teeth in false bravado. "Fine." He pushed out of the booth.

I expected a couple of the enforcers to accompany Luis but none did.

Javier watched his brother stalk across the club with narrowed eyes. Their dynamic was as old as time. Weaker younger brother coveted what powerful older brother had, and older brother had to continually put him in his place. It would end in blood as it always did. Until then, Luis would be his liability.

A liability I can exploit... A plan came together as I watched Luis angrily shove open the door and step outside.

I was bound by my orders so I couldn't approach Javier or his enforcers. But Luis technically wasn't one of the enforcers.

He's fair game.

Thrilled to have found a move in what felt like an impossible chess game, I reached into my pocket, retrieved a wad of crumpled bills, and tossed them down on the table. I stood and gave Donna a jerky wave.

She didn't look up from her conversation with the dominatrix.

Hoping I never had to see her or her watered-down drinks again, I stumbled through the club doors after my prey.

The icy wind felt amazing after the stuffiness of the club. Out of reflex, I opened my mouth and tasted the fresh air. It carried the unmistakable odor of blood and death. Several humans had died recently. I sniffed, wondering if they were casualties of the Z-virus or of Javier's gang. I couldn't tell and honestly didn't give a fuck. The only thing that mattered was my dancer wasn't among them.

I carefully scanned the parking lot. It was empty except for the driver of an SUV idling near the street and Luis.

The urge to shift and attack Javier's brother gripped me, but it was overridden by my programming. My handler had ordered me not to blow my cover, so letting my beast take over wasn't an option.

Luis was just opening the door to one of the black Mercedes parked near the front of the lot when I shambled up next to him.

"Can I get a ride?" I asked in a slurred voice.

The long-haired male spun around, his face wrinkling in disgust. "*Chinga tu madre.*" When I didn't move, he raised his fist as if to hit me.

"Put your hand down," I ordered, infusing my voice with power. Using compulsion was a gamble, but I'd sensed the latent was nowhere as strong as his brother.

Luis's arm dropped.

Relieved as fuck that my power play had paid off, I said, "You're under my control."

"I'm under your control," he echoed, his eyes going blank.

"Where is Dr. Hurran?"

"At one of the university labs."

"Which one?"

"*No sé.*"

There had to be dozens of labs on campus. "What else do you know about her location?"

"She's being moved to the Hacienda tomorrow."

I cursed, once the scientist was inside Javier's heavily fortified compound, she'd be much harder to get to. "What time is she being moved?"

"*No sé.*"

"How many will be in her escort?"

"*No sé.*"

I gritted my teeth in frustration. "Guess."

"Four or five."

I could tear through that in a hot minute. The tension I'd been carrying evaporated. I had the intel. I'd completed the mission. Now I needed to get my ass back to base and relay it to Jen, but first...

I stepped closer to Luis and yanked off my sunglasses. "Make sure your brother leaves Lee alone."

"Who's Lee?"

"The dancer he's putting the moves on." I motioned back at the club.

"*Imposible.* He wants her in his bed."

My vision darkened with rage. "That will never happen." *She's mine.* "Tell him to forget her."

Luis blinked at me. "He's already sent Miguel to pick her up."

The fuck? The enforcer had left the club just a few minutes earlier. *Shit.* "Call Miguel and tell him there's been a change in plan. Tell him to go back to the Hacienda without the dancer."

"Miguel and the other *sicarios* only follow my brother's orders," Luis said in an emotionless voice.

Cursing, I grabbed Luis's arm and stared down at the expensive watch on his wrist. *There's plenty of time to take care of Miguel and still make Jen's deadline.*

The sound of the SUV's engine shutting off rushed my decision. I turned back to Luis. "Forget about us having this conversation."

"*Sí,*" he said, blinking.

I shuffled away from Luis as a massive Lykos stepped out of the SUV. The motherfucker was huge—nearly as large as I was in my natural form. Although I could have easily made short work of the auburn-haired shifter, I was relieved when he headed for the club.

"Jen," I whispered, stumbling to the sidewalk. "I have the intel, but I need to protect a civilian from Javier."

My handler didn't respond. Although I sensed her, our connection was muted, and her emotions were unclear.

I tried again. "Handler."

No response.

Throughout the course of my miserable life, I'd passed through several handlers. Some treated me decently. Others abused the shit out of me. But every single one of them responded when I called for them. It was part of *their* programming.

Maybe I should've been more concerned about what was going on with Jen, but all I could think about was my dancer. Lee's house wasn't far from here.

Miguel might already be there.

Fuck it. If Jen and the other handlers were watching me, I'd give them some entertainment. Abandoning my drunk act, I ran across the street and ducked behind the liquor store. In the dank smelling darkness, I stripped off my clothes. Dropping my disguise, I did an all over body shake and expanded into my natural form. Then, I activated the unique cloaking properties of my skin that rendered me invisible and raced toward my mate's home.

I covered the distance in less than a minute. When I was a street away from her house, I passed a black Mercedes speeding through the neighborhood.

Miguel.

My orders prevented me from approaching him, but what if he approached me? Grinning, I darted into the middle of the road. As the vehicle barreled toward me, I hummed one of the songs from my mate's dance routine.

I confirmed Miguel's identity and shifted my hand and

arm. Then, milliseconds before the vehicle could smash into me, I drove my massive claw-tipped paw straight into the three-pointed-star Mercedes-Benz emblem on the front grille. The impact sent the vehicle somersaulting over my head.

It landed right-side up with a deafening crunch. Noxious odors of smoke and gasoline wafted from the wreckage as Miguel's unconscious body slumped into the rapidly deflating airbag. The enforcer wasn't picking up my mate or anyone else tonight.

As I shifted my uninjured paw back into a hand, a light from one of the houses across the street flicked on.

I should go. The threat to my mate had been dealt with, and my programming urged me to head to the army base to make my handler's deadline. And yet, a much stronger need had me looking down the street.

I still have time to see Lee.

If my handler or any other soldiers had been monitoring me, they would have swooped in to apprehend me long before now.

A thrill shot through me. *I'm truly off leash.* As long as I followed the previously given order to be back at base by four, I could do whatever the fuck I wanted. And I wanted only one thing...

Someone pounded on my door hard enough to shake the wood frame.

The sound tore me from my terrifying memories.

"Come out, sugar. No hiding in your room when there's free beer and single men to be had."

The breath I was holding came out in a rush.

Cami.

Wiping away my tears, I quickly pushed the knife into its hiding place and covered it with the plank.

"One of those single men just poured his free beer all over me," I shouted back at her.

"I hope you made him lick it off."

"Yeah, no. Give me a second." I hastily swapped the damp sweater for a black halter top and opened the door.

Cami stood in the hallway still wearing the teeny-tiny plaid skirt and white thigh-highs from her set at the club. She'd tied her white button-down shirt into a knot under her ample cleavage. It showcased her tanned abs and the dangly belly button ring that matched my own.

"Aren't you a sight for sore eyes," she swayed unsteadily, a vodka bottle dangling from between her fingers.

I laughed. "Couldn't wait to start the party?"

"Don't give me a hard time. My head is throbbing, and I feel like crap. Thank God the new girl drew the short straw. There was no way I could've danced back-to-back sets." She took a healthy gulp from the bottle.

"What do you mean?"

"The evil-bitch-of-the-West didn't bother gracing us with her presence. Max is livid."

Goosebumps ran down my arms. "Jess didn't show?"

"Nope. But the good news is, I think she finally crossed the line this time. Given the way Max flipped his lid, she can kiss her job goodbye."

Oh, God. It wasn't a prank.

The room spun. "I-I saw Jess outside the club." Before my legs could give out, I sat down on my bed. "Some guy had torn out her... her stomach..."

"What?"

My tongue thickened, making it hard to speak the words out loud. "Then she got up and came after me. I think... I think they were zombies."

Cami burst into laughter.

I rubbed my temples. "I know how it sounds."

She came over and sat down beside me. "It sounds like you've been working too hard. Are you sure you saw what you think you did?"

"Pretty sure." I grabbed the bottle from her hands and gulped. The vodka tasted like rubbing alcohol and left me sputtering.

Cami slapped me on the back so hard I nearly fell off the bed.

"Ouch." She was strong for her slight frame. Pole dancing made for killer biceps.

She flashed me a chastising look. "Remember, I'm the girl with the weird conspiracy theories."

No argument there. She was always trying to convince me of inane things like scientists at the army base were engineering animal-human hybrids.

Cami gave me a knowing look. "Don't you think it's more likely that Jess was punking you? Just yesterday, I overheard her telling one of her friends she was planning her best prank ever."

"Yeah." I took another sip. My hand shook so badly vodka spilled over the side of the bottle.

"She probably got the idea about zombies from the news. And you know how good she is with stage makeup."

I nodded. "That's what I thought, but why wouldn't she show for her set?"

Cami scoffed. "Who knows why that crazy bitch does what she does? Maybe she gets her kicks from having us all suffer through her horrible country routine. Maybe she went crazy with the special effects and couldn't clean up quickly enough."

I let out a weak laugh. "She did go all out with the blood and guts. She even wore creepy white contacts."

Cami pulled the bottle out of my lap and took a swig. "We gotta get her back for this. Any ideas?"

I shook my head. "I'll think of something epic."

Jess is going down.

"That's my girl." Cami rubbed her hand. "Damn, even my hand's gone numb."

"Maybe you're coming down with something." I felt her forehead. It was strangely cool to the touch.

"Maybe I'm dying from that stupid vaccine. I knew better than to trust the government. They probably put arsenic in it. China's been doing that for decades."

I rolled my eyes. "Okay, who's crazy now? And why did

you get the shot, anyway?" A government-mandated vaccination seemed exactly like the type of thing she'd boycott.

Cami scowled. "My sister's due any minute, and she told me I couldn't meet the baby until I got the vaccine."

"Quite the hostage negotiator, eh?"

"Yeah, that's my sister for you, but at least I don't have to bail her out of jail tonight."

I winced. "Touché. Well, technically I can't get Eden until tomorrow." I knew from experience the police wouldn't release her before her hearing.

"Sweet. That means you and I can enjoy the party." Cami pushed herself to her feet, wobbling on six-inch stilettos.

I eyed her too-pale face. "Are you sure you're up for this?"

"No." She glanced down at her arm and frowned. "But if tonight is my last night on earth, I'm going to get drunk and laid."

"That's the spirit," I said, smiling.

"You're coming too." She grabbed my arm.

I knew better than to argue with her in this mood. "Fine, but just for a little while. I'm tired."

"You can sleep when you're dead." Cami pulled me to my feet. "Now let's get this party started!"

"Not too much drinking. I have to work tomorrow," I pleaded as she dragged me out the door.

"Of course," she promised.

I should have known better.

Within a half an hour she'd bullied me into a drinking game with Reed, Ronnie, Morgan, and Scooter.

An hour later, my vision was hazy. Ronnie's lame jokes were getting funnier, and Scooter was getting better-looking.

Once the keg ran dry, the other partygoers cleared out. It left just the six of us sitting around the kitchen table along with Cami's almost empty vodka bottle and Gran's gin collection. An indie cover version of "When the Levee Breaks" was playing on Reed's vintage record player, the perfect sound-track for the Never Have I Ever drinking game we were playing.

Ronnie cleared his throat. Over the course of the night, his freckled face had taken on the hue of his cup. "Never have I ever had sex with two people at the same time."

The rest of the guys and I shook our heads.

Cami scoffed and took a healthy drink from her cup. "Come on. You're all losers. At this rate, I'll be too trashed to have sex with one of you guys." Her gaze rested briefly on Reed.

He pointedly ignored her as he'd been doing all night.

Feeling unexpectedly relieved that he wasn't interested in her subtle and not-so-subtle attempts at seduction, I grinned. "We can't all be skanky hos." I turned and winked at her. I must've moved too fast because I nearly fell off my chair.

Scooter caught my elbow to steady me.

Ronnie, who'd never taken his eyes off Cami, beamed in her direction. "You're my kind of woman."

Cami gave him a once-over and flashed him a thousand-watt smile. "But are you man enough for me?"

Oh, God, not Cami and Ronnie. That was a recipe for disaster. I met Reed's gaze across the table and rolled my eyes.

Instead of sharing my disgust, he wore a strained expression. "Hey guys, I think it's time to pack it in for the night."

I waved my hand at him dismissively. "Come on, we're having a good time."

Reed looked down at Scooter's hand holding my arm. "Jesus, woman. I've never seen you drink like this. You can barely sit upright in your chair."

Feeling self-conscious, I straightened in my seat. True, I wasn't much of a drinker. But I thought I was holding my own.

Scooter slid an arm over my shoulder. "What are you, her dad? She's just having fun. Lay off."

Reed tightened his grip around his plastic cup, nearly crushing it in half. Clearly, he wasn't having a good time, and it was his birthday.

Maybe we should cut the night short...

The rebel inside me flipped off that idea. It wasn't fair. I hadn't felt this light and free in forever. I was tired of always being the responsible one.

Didn't I deserve to live it up a little?

Scooter gave everyone at the table an assessing look. "Never have I ever had a Big Mac."

Cami gasped. "No way."

Scooter's face reddened. "Yeah, I have wheat and dairy allergies."

Ronnie slapped him on his back. "That's sad, man."

Everyone at the table knocked back their cups.

My eyes didn't even water. The vodka went down like apple juice at this point. Feeling bad for Scooter, I said. "I can't eat Big Macs either."

"Really?"

"Yeah. My sister is forcing us to eat vegan." I wrinkled my nose, thinking about the tofu sandwiches she'd made for lunch yesterday.

He chuckled. "How about I take you to the Red Dog Saloon for our first date? We'll have steak and your sister will be none the wiser."

Reed slammed his cup down on the table, gin sloshing across the top. If he glared any harder at Scooter, the college boy's head would've exploded.

What's up with him?

Trying to diffuse the tension, I shook off Scooter's arm. "My turn." I thought for a second, and then said, "Never have I ever been in love."

Reed held my gaze, tipped his cup to me, and slowly drank.

Feeling like a butterfly pinned to a wall, I swallowed hard. A quick glance around the table revealed everyone was drinking.

My mood bottomed out. *Is something wrong with me?*

An entire lifetime of choices rushed through my mind. Me rejecting Josh, the cute boy with dimples who'd asked me to the eighth-grade dance. Me spurning Darren, who'd stubbornly spent most of sophomore year trying to get me to go out with him. The countless faces of boys and men who'd asked me out in the years since then. I'd never regretted my decision to avoid all things male until that moment.

Scooter leaned over. "You just haven't met the right guy." He reached down and rubbed my jean-clad thigh.

Instead of pulling away like I normally would, I smiled. Maybe he was right. He was kind of sexy in that clean-cut, boy-next-door way. "Do you think you're Mr. Right?"

Scooter responded by dragging me into his lap.

I giggled, enjoying the feeling of a pair of arms around me. *Why have I been avoiding this my whole life?*

The sound of Reed gritting his teeth had me jerking my head up.

What's his deal tonight?

Next to me, Morgan swiped his dark hair out of his face and leveled the table with a serious look. "Never have I ever killed someone."

As his words registered, I felt the blood leaving my face.

"Trust Morgan to go to the dark side," joked Ronnie. "No one's going to drink to that."

Reed flashed me a quick, unfathomable look.

The kitchen spun around me. My stomach churned, and bile clawed its way up the back of my throat. I jumped off Scooter's lap and promptly crashed into the table.

One of the bottles fell over. The piney smell of gin filled the kitchen.

Morgan cursed and stared down at the growing wet spot in his lap.

Ronnie grabbed a wad of paper towels and started mopping up the spill. "Ms. Walker apparently can't handle her liquor."

"Are you okay?" Cami and Scooter asked at the same time.

I held my hand up to my mouth, afraid if I opened it, I'd start projectile vomiting.

"Dude, she's going to hurl." Morgan slid back from the table.

Scooter stood. "Come on, I'll take you to the bathroom."

Reed was suddenly standing between us. "You're not taking her anywhere, man."

The two men scowled at each other.

I stared at Reed in confusion. He never acted like this. He hated conflict. My stomach lurched again. There was no time to analyze his behavior. I took off down the hallway and made it to the bathroom just in time to spill my guts into the toilet.

After my stomach finally stopped spasming, I laid my head down on the floor.

The cool tile felt wonderful.

Someone rapped at the door a few minutes later. "Are you okay, sugar?"

"Yeah," I called back to Cami. "I just need a minute."

"Take your time. I've got someone to keep me company." She giggled.

"Not Ronnie. Please Cami, anyone except Ronnie," I pleaded, but she'd already walked away.

I don't know how long I lay there, but eventually I felt well enough to use the bathroom sink to pull myself up.

The face that stared back at me in the mirror made me cringe. My long hair was tangled around my pale, clammy face, and my eye makeup was smeared. Deciding to clean myself up, I brushed my teeth and took a long hot shower. The water felt amazing beating against my sore muscles and the sweet scent of my vanilla body wash burned away the smell of alcohol and vomit.

Oh, God. I should've stopped drinking an hour ago and I never should have played that stupid game. *What if the others noticed my reaction to Morgan's statement?*

My stomach rolled again.

Only Reed, Eden, and Uncle Duncan knew the dark truth about my past. And I needed it to stay that way. I turned the water off with a hard yank. Pissed that I let myself get into such a situation, I toweled off with a fervor that left my skin pink.

Then I grabbed a comb and ran it through my hair with punishing strokes.

Scooter had probably left by now. I wasn't sure if that was a good thing or a bad thing. His muscular arms had felt really nice around me.

What would his kiss feel like?

I brought my hand to my mouth and traced my fingers over my lips. I shivered, my nipples hardening.

I moved my hand down to my breasts. Passion sparked through me as I caressed them.

They'd been so swollen and achy tonight as if begging for someone's touch. For some reason, I thought of Javier. *What would it feel like to be with him?*

My breath caught as I slipped a finger between my legs.

Would he touch me like this?

Pleasure arced through me as I circled my clit.

Love I didn't need. Love led to pain. But maybe there could be lust.

What if I took Javier up on his offer? He's sexy as hell and he'd pay me forty grand for the weekend.

I put one foot on the edge of the counter and imagined his amber eyes looking up at me as he licked and sucked me senseless. I felt myself drawing tighter and tighter like a bow about to snap. I moved my fingers frantically over my nub, chasing an orgasm that was so... very... close...

Someone knocked on the door.

I froze, hoping whoever it was would go away.

"Lee, are you okay?"

It's Reed. Crap. My cleft throbbed with a deep pressure that left me feeling frustrated.

"Lee?"

"I'm fine. Leave me alone." *Maybe he'll go away so I can finish.*

"Can you open the door?"

I glared at him through the wood. "No. Go away."

"Lee, please."

Annoyed, I brought my leg down, toga-wrapped myself in a towel, and jerked the door open. "What is so goddamn important I can't get a moment to myself?"

❧ II ❧

REED

The sight of Lee fresh from the shower stole my breath.

She was ravishing with or without makeup, but dressed in only a damp towel she was the sexiest thing I'd ever seen.

I quickly took mental snapshots of the water dripping down her flushed skin.

Lee flipped her wet hair back, and her towel unknotted. She grabbed the sides of the terry cloth before it could completely fall open, but what I'd glimpsed made my head spin.

Jesus. My mouth opened and closed as my mind short-circuited.

"What do you want?"

Her irritated tone ripped me from my mental paralysis.

Why is she annoyed with me? She's the one acting like an idiot.

The memory of her cuddling with Scooter made me want to punch my fist through a wall. Lee had never shown an interest in any guy before and to see her wrapped in that tool's arms gutted me. As far as I could tell, Scooter was as deep as a puddle and as smart as a bag of weed.

But what if he is her type?

I rejected that idea. Earlier this year, I'd overheard her talking with Cami about her ideal man. I'd made sure I ticked off all her boxes.

Tall. Check.

Long hair. Check.

Tattoos. Check.

And there had been one other qualification. Checking off that box had been painful as hell, but she was worth it.

Scooter didn't meet her criteria, and the muscle-bound gorilla had the nerve to argue with me when I asked him to go. Normally, I tried not to let anything bother me, but I'd told him in no uncertain terms that if he didn't leave, I'd throw him the fuck out.

He'd stepped up into my face and tried to use his bigger size to intimidate me, only to find that I don't intimidate easy. Although I was usually a proponent of peaceful resolutions, all bets were off when it came to Lee.

I'd fight for her. Hell, I'd kill for her.

Scooter must've seen that in my eyes, because he'd backed away and headed out the door.

Good fucking riddance.

Lee's sound of annoyance dragged my attention back to our conversation. "Did you have something to say, or are you just going to stand there?" She kicked her discarded clothes at my head.

I ducked. "Jesus, woman. I thought this would make you feel better." I held up a blue sports drink as if it were a peace offering.

"Oh." Her angry expression faded. "Thanks." She grabbed the drink, pushed past me, and padded into her room across the hall.

Not allowing her to dismiss me so easily, I followed her into her room and closed the door behind us. Not that we needed the privacy.

I'd sent everyone home except Cami and Ronnie, who were currently getting their freak on in the living room. I really hoped they stayed off the furniture. Just thinking about sitting in their wet spot made me want to hurl.

Lee sat down on her bed and took a deep gulp of the sports drink.

Good. She needed the electrolyte replacement after all the liquor she'd had.

What is she thinking getting that drunk?

Lee set the bottle down on the floor, tension rolling off of her. "Do you think any of our friends realized..." Her voice went tight.

It took me a moment to catch her meaning. *Is that what she's worried about?* "Hell no. They don't have a clue. They just thought your night of slamming shots caught up to you."

She let out a relieved sigh.

Once again, I tried to puzzle out why she'd acted so out of character tonight.

Lee's gaze narrowed. "Why are you staring at me like that?"

"I'm worried about you. Normally, you're the one keeping it together while we all go crazy. What's going on?"

Lee glanced away as she finger-combed her hair. "I just wanted to cut loose a little. Instead of giving me a hard time, why don't you enjoy the rest of your birthday party?"

"I sent everyone home. Well, everyone but Cami and Ronnie. They're too trashed to drive and they seem to want to get to know one another better." I hid my inward shudder.

She snorted. "I can't think of two people who'd be worse for each other."

"I can. You and that Scooter guy. What the hell was up with that?"

She glanced away, a guilty look on her face.

It was that expression that cut me deepest. *She doesn't even know why she was all over that guy.* I shut my mouth before I blurted out the question I really wanted to ask. *Why him and not me?*

She took a deep breath. "It's none of your business. Why were you being such a dick to him, anyway?"

We were stepping through dangerous territory. While I fumbled for an answer, I stared at the top of her dresser. Gran's collection of porcelain frogs cavorted across the mahogany finish. I'd always liked those frogs. I should write a song about them someday.

"Reed, are you even listening to me?"

"Yeah. That poser didn't deserve you, and he was out of line."

"Really? He didn't pinch my ass once." She let out a husky laugh that told me she was still buzzed.

I sat down next to her, forcing my gaze from lingering on her bare, damp legs. "You've never shown an interest in any guy before."

She crossed her arms over her chest. "I'm not gay."

"I never thought you were." I'd caught her staring at my ass more than a dozen times this week alone. "But you've always avoided the dating scene."

"You're one to talk. You've never even gone on a date." Her gaze went to my chest, and she flushed.

I rubbed my scars through the fabric of my shirt. I was embarrassed about the way I looked, but that's not why I avoided dating. The urge to confess everything made my throat tight.

Now isn't the right time.

Aubry's story about her mother flashed in my mind.

What if I lose Lee to some other dude while I wait for the right time?

Taking a deep breath, I said, "Yeah, but not for the reason you think. I've been waiting for someone."

She blinked. "Really? Who?"

Here it is. The moment I'd been both dreading and anticipating for years.

Do I go for it or do I play it safe?

My mouth dried, and my heart started to pound.

Seeming to grow impatient with my tongue-tied silence, Lee reclined back on her bed. "Fine, keep your secrets. As for me, maybe I'm just tired of being alone."

"You're not alone." I'd never leave her side.

"I know. I have you and Eden, but it's not the same thing. God. I can't believe I'm actually going to say this, but I think… I think I'm ready to hook up with someone. You should too. You're gorgeous, Reed. You could have had your pick of the women at the party tonight."

"I don't want them." I shifted across the bed so I was stretched out next to her.

"Well, who then?" Her beautiful caramel-colored eyes were filled with questions. Questions I was finally going to answer.

The staccato hammering of my heart roared in my ears.

Screw it. Here goes nothing.

"You." I leaned over and kissed her.

She gasped.

I deepened the kiss, tasting her shock along with spearmint toothpaste.

She moved her mouth against mine and moaned my name. My motherfucking name.

Thank Jesus!

She shuddered at the first stroke of my tongue against hers and pulled me down over her.

All the blood in my body shot straight between my hips as the softest parts of her pressed against the hardest parts of me.

Can this really be happening?

She let out a sexy moan and bit down on my lower lip.

My head spun as if I'd smoked an entire bowl of that trippy weed Ronnie made me try on my last birthday. If this was a hallucination, I never wanted it to end. Not with the incredible feeling of her gorgeous body under me.

I tore my mouth from hers and kissed down the delicate arch of her neck, cataloging every sharp inhale and gasp.

All of my senses intensified. Her skin had never felt so soft, and the scent of her vanilla body wash had never seemed more seductive.

I lapped at a tiny drop of forgotten water that had collected in the recesses of her collarbone.

She let out a husky moan, her fingers threading through my hair.

As I kissed down the top of her chest, her breathing quickened. Coming to the terry cloth barrier, I looked into her hooded gaze, seeking permission.

In response, she reached between us and yanked open the towel.

The sight of all that bare golden skin blanked my mind. My need ignited in a raw, brutal explosion of hunger so desperate it took all my self-control not to fall over her in a frenzy. "I've been dreaming about this... about you forever."

Some of the heat left her gaze.

Is she having second thoughts?

She chewed her lower lip the way she always did when she was anxious. "Maybe this isn't—"

Sensing that her excitement was fading, I lowered my head and licked one of her stiff brown nipples.

She let out a raspy moan.

Encouraged, I licked and sucked its twin.

She threw her head back against the pillows. "Oh, God. Yes, more."

I spent the next few minutes experimenting with different levels of suction and pressure.

She rocked her hips under mine in a wordless plea for me to shift my attention.

When I still didn't switch my focus, she grabbed my hand and placed it between her legs. "Touch me here."

My motherfucking mind was blown.

Her bare pussy was even more beautiful than it'd been in my fantasies.

When I didn't move, she rubbed herself against my hand. "Please."

Thanking every god I'd ever heard of under my breath, I slowly stroked her. It was so much hotter and sexier than the erotic videos I watched on my phone at night.

I switched the angle of my fingers to press against the top of her sex.

She cried out and nearly flew off the bed.

I went still thinking I'd done something wrong, but she rocked against my hand, urging me on.

Gaining more confidence, I rubbed her little nub harder and faster.

"Oh, yes!" she moaned brokenly.

My dick strained at my zipper. It was a furious, throbbing ache that grew more uncomfortable with every breath. Guided by some primitive playbook, I slid two fingers into her.

Her inner muscles clamped around my fingers. She was so hot, wet, and impossibly tight.

My breathing went ragged as I finger fucked her.

"God, yes. More." Her hips worked furiously as she bucked against my hand.

I wanted her to come all over my fingers, but I wanted to taste her orgasm even more. I pulled my hand away and kissed down her stomach.

"Yes," she cried, her legs sawing under me. When I stopped to nuzzle her belly button ring, she let out a frustrated cry and shoved my face between her legs.

Chuckling, I gripped her hips and brought my mouth to her center. Then, I set about making the woman of my dreams come harder than she ever had in her life.

LEE

Nothing had ever felt as incredible as the velvet heat of Reed's mouth. All I could do was quiver and shake as pleasure overwhelmed me.

He made a humming sound. The vibration sent me into yet another stratosphere of pleasure.

Who knew Reed was so talented with his lips?

His scent—clove with a hint of juniper spice from the gin—surrounded me. It was familiar and yet strange at the same time.

An inner voice whispered a warning. Before I could register it, Reed thrust his tongue deep inside me.

My thoughts scattered like confetti in the wind. "Yes, there!" I cried, arching off the bed.

As he went to work licking every inch of my core, I wrapped my legs around his shoulders and rocked against his face. His beard rasped against the skin of my inner thighs, but I barely felt the burn.

Lust and alcohol spun me into dizzying bliss. "God, yes. More." Pressure coiled tighter and tighter inside me.

A loud thunk sounded by my window.

Reed froze and looked up. "Did you hear that?"

"Don't stop." I grabbed the back of his head and ground myself against his lips.

"I should have known you'd be bossy in the bedroom, too." The sound of his laugh threatened to kick down the door of a lifetime of memories.

This is wrong.

Reed is family.

He can't be my lover…

Screw that. Forcing all thoughts except pleasure away, I arched off the bed, chasing his mouth.

Hearing my unspoken plea, he spread my thighs wider and began licking me hard and fast.

I thrashed against his mouth, overcome with mind-blowing pleasure. As I spiraled higher and higher, it became impossible to breathe. To think.

He fixed his mouth around my clit and sucked hard.

Letting out a shriek, I detonated into the most intense orgasm of my life. My vision dimmed before coming back into full focus.

Reed looked up at me from between my legs. "Did that feel good?"

There weren't words for how good. Trembling with the aftershocks, all I could do was nod.

He pushed himself up on his arms. "I've never done that before, but I've been studying."

I blinked up at him. "Studying?"

"Yeah." His face flushed. "I've kinda been waiting for this moment all my life."

My blissed out and inebriated mind reeled in shock at his confession.

"This is the best birthday present ever." He punctuated his words by lowering his head and licking my clit again.

Ecstasy blindsided me. All I could do was moan and fist

the covers as he brought me to orgasm a second time. I came so hard I swear the curtains over my window undulated with my screams. After I'd melted into a puddle of pure rapture, he crawled over my body.

"I've been waiting for something else too," he whispered in my ear.

"Mmm-hmm." I'd totally lost track of our conversation.

"This." His hard, lean muscles pressed me into the softness of the mattress as he settled his hips between my thighs. His hard cock pressed against my aching sex.

My greedy clit pulsed with renewed hunger. She needed more.

More touching.

More pleasure.

More Reed.

The desire to feel his skin against mine had me grabbing his shirt. "Take this off." My voice was so husky, I almost didn't recognize it.

Reed rocked back on his knees, his hands going to the top button of his shirt. A mixture of emotions flashed across his face.

He didn't think his scars would bother me. Did he? "Here, let me." I pushed myself up. The mattress seemed to rock underneath me like Reed's waterbed. *I must still be drunk.* I put a hand against his chest to steady myself.

His heart pounded a furious beat under the fabric of his shirt.

Our eyes met.

"No," he mumbled. "You don't need to see this." His warm palm curled around my hand.

I brushed it away. "You've just fucked me with your tongue. The least you can do is take your shirt off."

"Lee," he pleaded.

I wouldn't let his insecurity kill this moment. Holding his

gaze, I slowly unbuttoned his shirt. When I finally swept the fabric aside, I let out a shocked gasp.

Despite us living together for years, he'd always kept his scars hidden. Hell, he even swam in a long sleeve shirt. Now, seeing the overwhelming extent of damage, I could see why.

How did he survive this?

Tears welled in my eyes as I realized how much pain he must've suffered.

"Great. I'm making you cry." Reed clenched his jaw and tried to close his shirt.

"Don't hide from me." I yanked it all the way off and tossed it on the floor.

Reed looked down at himself and flinched. "I'm a freak."

"No, you're not." There was no denying the scars were intense. I swept my hands over his chest. The burn scars covering his chest and arms were almost like braille under the pads of my fingertips. Lower, along his abdomen were the smooth silvery scars from the shrapnel that had impaled him in the accident. They mingled with the thicker, raised incision scars from the multiple surgeries that saved his life.

His breath caught, and he stared down at me. It seemed like he was desperately trying to read me.

I bent my head and began kissing each scar.

He groaned as I licked one of the burn scars that warped the flesh of his nipple. "You don't have to do th—"

He broke off when I kissed him lower. When I got to his waistband, he shuddered and fell back onto the bed. "Jesus, woman. I don't think I'll be able to hold back if you put your mouth on me."

"Maybe I don't want you to hold back." While he watched with wide eyes, I undid the top button of his fly and slid the zipper down.

In contrast to the scarred flesh of his upper body, the bronze skin below his waist was kissably smooth.

With a tug, I slid off his boxer briefs. His thick shaft sprung out and bobbed in the air inches from my lips. "Oh, my!" I reared back in shock.

I'd seen my fair share of penises. Hell, I couldn't get through a week at the club without some perv whipping out his junk during a private show, but I'd seen nothing quite like this.

"What the——?" I stared, slack-jawed, at the rows of silver barbells that pierced the underside of his cock from head to base.

"It's called a Jacob's ladder. Do you like it?"

Transfixed, I ran my fingers over the barbells. "It looks painful."

He shuddered, and his thick purple crown grew slick with arousal. "I won't lie. It hurt like a son of a bitch."

"Was this the reason you walked like a drunken cowboy for weeks on end?"

"Yeah," he gasped, rocking against my fingers.

"Why would you do this?" Some dancers at the club had nipple piercings, and I even knew one dancer who had her clit pierced, but they did it to enhance their sexual pleasure. Reed was just as sexually inexperienced as I was.

"I did it for you."

"Me?"

"Yeah, I overheard you telling Cami that you love men with pierced cocks."

"What?" I blinked in confusion. "I never said that——" A distant memory tugged at the back of my mind. "Are you talking about the time when Cami tried to set me up with Leo?"

Reed gave me a puzzled look.

Oh, God. "Reed, I was joking." For some inane reason, Cami had been trying to set me up with her ex-boyfriend. Knowing Leo was pierced, I'd said sarcastically that my ideal man was tall, long-haired, tattooed, and had a pierced cock.

I'd had no idea that Reed was eavesdropping. And even if I'd known, I'd never imagine he'd take my words seriously and do something so insane.

"What do you mean?"

"I mean, I was just kidding about wanting someone pierced."

Reed's blue eyes widened. "You mean... you mean..." His erection deflated. "Jesus, I feel like the biggest fucking idiot right now."

I couldn't take my eyes from the barbells. "I can't believe you'd do something so crazy... so painful..."

He dragged in a deep breath. "Isn't it obvious, woman? I love you. I always have."

The raw emotion in his gaze took my breath away.

He loves me.

Wait. What? No. My inner alarm shrieked. This was supposed to be fun. No emotional attachments. Passionate love made people crazy. I saw my mother's lifeless body in my mind's eye.

I sat up in bed. "This isn't happening."

"What?"

"Leave."

"But..." His face twisted with confusion and pain.

"Just go now," I said so loudly the mirror over my dresser shook and the curtains over my window fluttered.

Reed slid off the bed and bent down to grab his pants.

Oh, God. He had the finest ass of any man I'd ever seen. Forcing my gaze away, I threw my comforter over myself.

"We'll act like this never happened." Things could go back to the way they were.

Reed shook his head. "I can't do that. I love you."

I scooted back on the bed until my spine hit the headboard. "Reed, I love you too—"

"I knew it. I knew you felt the sam—"

"—like a brother," I lied softly. "Even though we aren't blood siblings, I'll always think of you that way." It wasn't true, but I needed him out before we did something we could never come back from.

"What about..." He motioned between us.

I tugged the comforter tighter around me. "A mistake."

His eyes narrowed. "You liked me touching you. I know you did."

I opened my mouth to deny it but couldn't. "Just leave."

"If I did or said anything to upset you—"

I interrupted him. "You didn't. Just go."

His shoulders slumped, and he turned toward the door.

"Don't go anywhere, cocksucker," a deep raspy voice ordered.

Reed spun around at the same time a huge, naked man emerged from behind my curtains.

Certain the guy was an alcohol induced hallucination. I closed my eyes and opened them again. The man was still there.

No, my shocked mind amended as I stared into his glowing yellow eyes. *Not a man. A monster.* A nearly ten-foot monster with jagged fangs and rippling muscles that enveloped every inch of his body down to the massive erection he sported between his brawny thighs.

I opened my mouth to scream.

The monster brought one of his fingers to his lips. "Neither of you move or make a sound." His voice rang with an otherworldly tone that reverberated inside my head.

I tried to bolt from the bed and found I couldn't move a muscle.

Oh, God! What's happening? Fear skittered down my spine.

Reed was a statue next to my bed. His terror-filled eyes were wide. "Run," he mouthed.

"I can't," I mouthed back. My breath came in sharp, shallow, pants. Somehow the monster was in total control. *What will he do to us?*

As if reading my mind, the monster bared his fangs in a smile made of nightmares.

❧ 13 ❧

HUNTER

My dancer and her roommate stared at me with mirroring looks of horror. The frantic pounding of their heartbeats rang in my ears, while the acrid tang of their fear burned my nostrils.

Normally, I'd eat that terror and pain up like a pancake breakfast, but not when it was coming from her.

My mate.

I wanted her to look at me the way she had back in the club. I wanted her to look at me the way she was looking at that human.

Snarling, I scowled at Reed.

Color leeched from his tanned face. To his credit, he didn't flinch from my gaze, but I sensed his rising panic and desire to protect my mate. It was the only reason he still drew breath.

When I'd first arrived at the house, I'd been enraged to scent a male's arousal through her open window.

Driven nearly insane with fury, I'd dove through the window, intent on eviscerating my rival.

But then I'd clawed the curtain open and found my mate

stretched out on her bed with her roommate's face trapped between her thighs. *Her gay roommate.*

Shocked, I'd struggled to make sense of what I was seeing.

From weeks of stalking Lee, when I was supposed to be watching Javier, I knew everything about them. I'd seen the way Reed rejected every female who made a pass at him, and I'd seen the way my dancer bossed him around like a younger brother.

The two of them screwing didn't make sense. What did make sense was that she was still under Javier's compulsion and she'd jumped the first available male her age. It was a testament to her beauty and allure that not even the gay roommate could resist her.

I still wanted to kill him for touching what was mine, but I also knew he was part of her family unit and she'd be devastated at losing him.

This was lost on my beast who thrashed under my skin, trying to take control. *Kill him! Mate her!* Breathing hard, I fought to stay in control. I knew if I fully shifted, I'd end up murdering them both.

"More! More!" My dancer's cries drew my attention to the bed where they writhed together. Her thighs were spread around that cocksucker's face as he licked and sucked her the way I longed to do.

Transfixed, I crouched down, watching him run his tongue along her plump lips with more enthusiasm than skill. The sight of her bare pussy gleaming with her lust and his saliva electrified me.

No doubt my bio readings were lit up like a fucking Christmas tree. Thank fuck my handler had gone MIA.

Groaning under my breath, I'd watched as my mate bucked against his mouth, digging her hands into the back of his head.

All at once, my murderous rage shifted into a desperate

hunger. I dropped my hand to my throbbing cock. With her wild cries in my ears and the sweet scent of her lust burning my nostrils, I stroked myself.

The barbs along my shaft shredded the skin of my palm, but I welcomed the pain. It grounded me just enough to keep the beast at bay, and the blood acted as a lubricant. Shutting my eyes, I imagined I was thrusting into her hot, wet heat.

Pleasure blanked my mind as the coppery smell of my blood mixed with the scent of her passion.

Her cries increased in intensity until she gave one more keening wail.

I came with a muffled roar. Hot ribbons of blood and cum splattered the curtains as I pumped out my release. The moment I regained my senses, I cringed at the mess I'd made.

Fuck. I couldn't even jack off without creating a crime scene. Cursing under my breath, I shifted my hand to a paw, at the same time moving the curtains aside to glimpse my mate. My claws shredded the fabric to ribbons.

Snarling, I shifted my paw into a fully healed human hand and peered through the tattered strips of cloth.

Although Reed was clearly inexperienced, my mate didn't seem to care as she smiled up at him.

Envy raked over me.

I can't touch her like he can. My claws would rip through her soft skin.

I can't kiss her like he can. The poison dripping from my fangs would kill her.

I can't mate her like he can. My barbed cock would shred her pussy.

As I watched her undress him, a forbidden thought flashed into my mind. *Why not possess him?*

I shook my head, rejecting the idea. Ghost had made me swear never to use that dark gift. He'd warned me the use of it would bring about my death, and only a fool ignored his prophesies.

And yet... Never had I been more tempted to use the abilities I'd discovered by accident. During one of my previous handler's conditioning, aka torture, sessions, I'd literally had an out-of-body experience. I'd been in so much pain my consciousness had briefly escaped my body and flown into a human soldier sleeping in the barracks nearby. I'd possessed him long enough to stumble outside and stare at the full moon.

But my soul jump, as Ghost called it, made my biometrics go crazy, which hadn't gone unnoticed by my prior handler. He'd sent me back to the lab for testing. The experiments I'd had to undergo there made my handler's conditioning sessions seem like a good time. I'd spent months in the lab and was lucky to make it out at all.

But no one is monitoring me now...

My mate's angry shout tore me from my internal debate. With a jolt of surprise, I realized she was telling Reed to go, and the cocksucker was actually leaving.

Fuck. If he went away, so did my opportunity to be with her.

No!

Before I could consider the ramifications, I'd thrown back the curtain and revealed myself.

And here we are.

I wet my lips knowing I could order him to fuck her every which way from Sunday and he'd do it while I watched.

But I was done watching. I cleared my throat. "You're under my control." While Reed and my mate blinked slowly in acquiescence, I uttered another order. "Reed, go to sleep."

On his next breath, the cocksucker's eyes closed, and he passed out on the ground.

My mate let out a cry.

"Lee, forget the last ten minutes," I commanded. Then I turned and knelt behind her curtain.

Having no recollection of me now, my mate's attention fixed on her unconscious roommate. "Reed!"

I heard her scramble off the bed, no doubt checking on him.

With one last look out the window at her empty back-yard, I shut my eyes and pushed my consciousness out of my body just like I'd done all those years ago. There was a moment of disorientation as I turned incorporeal, but I locked on my target and flew straight into Reed's mouth. In less than a second, I took control of his body.

"Reed?"

Snapping my borrowed eyes open, I stared up into my mate's face. Even without the heightened sensitivity of my natural vision, she looked stunning.

I leaned closer and inhaled deeply. Reed's dull human senses couldn't pick up the intoxicating scent of her pheromones. But she still smelled incredible.

"Are you okay?" Her wide brown eyes shone with emotion that made my new human heart beat faster.

Blood pooled in my cock, which pulsed with a desperate need to be inside her. Trying to ignore the ache, I caressed the curve of her jaw.

"So soft," I murmured, finding the smooth sound of my borrowed voice a little jarring. "My dirty dancer."

"Reed?" she whispered. "Your eyes..."

I cupped the back of her head and brought her mouth down on mine. Then I kissed her with all the passion burning inside me.

Tentatively, her tongue moved against mine.

It was all the encouragement I needed. Groaning against her lips, I slid my hands down to her breasts. They were perfect—soft, yet firm, and large enough to overfill these human hands.

She moaned as I rolled her nipples between my fingers.

After inhaling her sounds of pleasure, I licked my way down her neck.

She tried to pull away. "Ah... I don't think..."

Sensing her rising desire, I drew her nipple into my mouth.

"Oh, God!" She swayed and fell back on the floor, her leg knocking over an open bottle of Gatorade.

I followed her down, not breaking suction for a second.

The blue liquid coated us as I worked her nipples into stiff points, but I didn't give a fuck. We could have been burning alive at that point and I wouldn't have cared as long as I could keep touching her... tasting her.

Rising above her, I spread her thighs open with my knees. Then, grabbing her ass in my hands, I lifted her pussy to my mouth.

She let out a broken gasp, her pupils blown with shock and desire.

Ah, fuck. She was as sweet as I'd imagined. I lapped at her cream before biting down on her clit.

She instantly came apart, shaking like a rag doll in my arms.

I slid a finger inside, finding her hot and so very wet.

Unable to wait any longer, I grabbed my borrowed cock and positioned it at her entrance. Although it was large for a human, she'd been primed well.

She can take it.

Her slumberous eyes widened. "Reed—"

I placed my forefinger on her mouth to silence her. I didn't want any other male's name on her lips.

"I want to claim you, dirty dancer." I ran my cock up and down her sex, bathing it in her honey until it glistened.

She shuddered.

"Do you want that?" I asked, flicking her clit with my thumb.

She let out a broken moan.

"Answer me," I demanded. I was crossing a dangerous line already. As excruciating as it would be to walk away, I would if she didn't truly want this. But I sensed she did.

"Yes," she hissed, opening her thighs wider.

Thank fuck. Bracing her ass in my hands, I slammed balls-deep into her.

She was so tight, my eyes crossed.

Her muffled cry told me what my body had already figured out.

She's a virgin. Was a virgin.

I froze and glanced at her face.

Her expression was strained, and her lower lip was caught between her teeth. "I-it hurts a little. Maybe it's the barbells."

Some primal instinct urged me to rectify her discomfort ASAP. I reached my hand between us and rubbed her swollen clit. "Better."

"Ah!" She moved against my fingers. "That feels... good."

I let her rock against my cock until the tension left her body and her moans filled the room.

Lust strung me as tight as a drum, but I refused to move until she came. She'd have a good fucking memory of her first time, even if it killed me.

"I'm close!" she cried. Her face was flushed and contorted into an expression halfway between anguish and euphoria.

I worked her nub harder.

She came with a scream.

The feeling of her hot flesh clamping down on me made my self-control snap. Growling, I fell over her, thrusting hard and fast.

Her body surged under mine as she raked my back with her long nails.

Giving myself over to the frenzied need to mate her, I dropped my head to the side of her neck and pistioned into her.

Our bodies, slicked with sweat and fucking Gatorade, slapped together.

Her cries became louder and louder until she came with a wild shriek.

Howling her name, I spilled deep inside her spasming pussy. Then I collapsed over her, my mind blown to smithereens.

She panted underneath me. "That was... that was..."

"Only the beginning." I flipped her onto her hands and knees.

"Again?" she gasped. Her thighs trembled as I positioned myself between them.

"And again and again," I promised, driving into her. It would take far more than one mating to ease my cravings for her.

Over the next two hours, I took her on her hands and knees twice and then up against the wall. We moved to the dresser where we fucked until one of her trinkets smashed to the ground. At her sad cry, I tossed her on the bed and licked her pussy until she forgot about the broken frog. Only when she'd passed out with a blissful smile on her face, did I finally allow her to rest.

I didn't want to sleep though. I wanted her again. I'd never get enough of her.

She's mine.

My mate.

I wiped a sweat-dampened lock of her hair off her shoulder and examined the soft pads of my fingers. In this body, I hadn't hurt her... well, beyond taking her virginity.

A wide grin of satisfaction crossed my face. I'd been her first, and I wanted to be her last. *But how could I stay with her?* The answer was that I couldn't stay with her, but Reed could.

I can stay in his body permanently.

The idea was at once alarming and exhilarating. All my life I'd fantasized about escaping my handlers and gaining my freedom. *This is my chance.* I'd take Lee somewhere safe. Somewhere we could make a life together.

No sooner had I made my decision to stay than I felt my consciousness being drawn out of Reed's body.

"No!" I tried to fight it, but it was as if my soul was being swept into a cyclone that sucked me up and deposited me back in my own wretched body.

Gut-wrenching pain hit me as soon as I opened my eyes. Clutching my head, I pleaded, "Stop!"

"Now you talk to me, motherfucker," Jen shrieked in my ear. Her anger, sharp and bright, pulsed through our bond. "I've been trying to reach you for the last hour. It's after four in the morning. Get your AWOL ass back to base right fucking now."

I stared at Lee, feeling all hope for our future slip away. "No. I—"

"Are you refusing a direct order? I'll end you right here and now." The pain intensified to the point I thought my head would explode.

Fuck! I tried to soul jump back into Reed but couldn't. Trapped by the escalating agony, I whispered, "I'll be back."

Thinking my words were for her, Jen sniffed. "Good, and you better have the intel on Dr. Hurran."

"I do," I gasped. As I dragged myself out of my mate's window and headed back to my handler, I cursed the fates for giving me a taste of heaven only to rip it away.

❧ 14 ❧

LEE

A loud shriek ripped me from sleep.

What the hell?

Cracking my eyes open, I peered at the bright light filtering through my half open curtains. As my mind slowly rebooted, I heard another loud cry from out in the living room. *Ugh. Cami and Ronnie are going at it early.*

With a sigh, I rolled out of bed as gracefully as a three legged-cat and half fell into the congealed blue puddle on the floor. As I glanced down at my sticky feet, I realized two things. First, my body ached in places it never had before. Second, Reed was sleeping in my bed. Naked.

Holy crap.

Memories of our night together hit me like a freight train. I glanced around the room, replaying our drunken sexcapade. The floor. The wall. The dresser. The bed. My face heated as I remembered all the things he'd done to me and the things I'd done to him.

Oh. My. God.

We'd screwed our platonic relationship right out the

window. There could be no going back. Not when my core throbbed with the imprint of his pierced cock.

I shivered, remembering how my shy, easy-going roommate had become a sex god last night. In turn, I'd become a nymphomaniac who'd taken everything he'd given me and demanded more.

But it hadn't just been the sex that had awoken something primal and raw inside me. There'd also been an undeniable connection between us that had only grown stronger the more times we'd come together.

Reed is in love with me.

And I... I...

Feelings I normally kept deep in the recesses of my soul threatened to overwhelm me. I pushed them away. It didn't matter what I felt, what we'd done was wrong.

He's family.

I wanted so badly to hit an undo button and erase last night. But Reed wasn't some stranger I'd had a one-night stand with. I couldn't just avoid ever seeing him again.

He'll want a relationship.

My chest tightened with so much anxiety I could barely breathe.

Another hair-raising shriek rang out.

Reed bolted upright in bed. "Jesus, what's that?"

"Cami and Ronnie," I said, spitting out their names. "They apparently want the entire neighborhood to know they're having sex."

His blue eyes alighted on me and widened. "You're naked." He glanced down at his scarred chest. "I'm naked." He looked back at me, his gaze filled with questions. "Did we... um... last night?"

I stared at him, dumbfounded.

He doesn't remember?

I knew he'd been drinking, but there was no way he could

have taken me so many times if he'd been amnesia-level drunk. Right?

Maybe he's just pretending.

For some reason, that thought made me self-conscious. I reached for his flannel shirt on the floor by my closet door and put it on. "What's the last thing you remember?"

"You told me to leave." His brow furrowed as if he was concentrating hard. "And there was a monster..." Blood drained from his face as he looked toward my window. "...with fangs and glowing eyes."

"A monster?" I repeated incredulously.

"Yeah, that sounds a little crazy. I-I don't remember anything after that." He rubbed one of the scratches my nails had made down his back. "Can you catch me up?"

Maybe it's the best thing if I 'forget' too. "I don't remember anything either." I chewed my lower lip, hoping he'd buy the lie.

He took a deep breath, no doubt inhaling the unmistakable scent of sex that perfumed the room. "Lee, it's obvious we slept together."

Oh, there wasn't much sleeping involved.

A loud crash from the front of the house saved me from addressing the seismic shift in our relationship. Ridiculously relieved to have a reason to leave, I reached for the door handle.

"What are you doing?"

"Going to tell Ronnie and Cami to keep it down."

The sound of glass breaking made me see red. *They better not be destroying my living room as part of their fuck fest.*

Reed jumped off the bed. "Our friends wouldn't trash the house."

Having his lean, muscular body only inches away from mine, made my lower belly clench and my breathing go ragged. Unable to fight the impulse, I swayed closer. *Has he always smelled this good?*

"We should call the police." He bent down to pick up his pants from the floor.

Seeing the half-moon marks my nails had left in his tight ass raised my body temperature ten degrees.

"Damn. My phone is dead." He frowned at the black device in his hands and threw on his jeans. "I'll check it out. Wait here."

"You're being ridiculous."

Ignoring me, he opened the door.

Trying not to admire how amazing he looked with his jeans riding low on his hips, I followed him into the hallway. He slipped into his bedroom and reemerged a few seconds later with a baseball bat.

I rolled my eyes. "Is that really necessary?"

Another crash sounded from the front room.

"Motherfuckers." I pushed past Reed and rushed down the hallway.

"Lee, wait!" Reed shouted, following close on my heels.

We skidded to a stop at the entryway to the living room.

The vertical blinds were open and the floor-to-ceiling windows bathed the space in bright light. It took several seconds for my eyes to adjust and even longer for my brain to make sense of the chaos in front of me.

Gran's antique floor lamp had been knocked over. The glass coffee table was shattered. The recliner was lying on its side. And blood... blood was everywhere.

Reed tightened his grip on the bat. "Jesus. What happened here?"

Wide-eyed, all I could do was take a hesitant step into the room.

The scent of blood was so strong that I tasted it in the

back of my throat. A river of it flowed from behind the couch.

With my heart in my throat, I peered around the armrest.

Cami, naked as the day she was born, was crouched over an equally naked Ronnie. Her mouth was latched around his throat. She was making soft slurping sounds.

"Cami, what are you doing?"

She glanced up. Blood dripped down her mouth and chin, giving her a creepy clown-like appearance.

I stumbled back, my mouth dropping open in horror.

She was abnormally pale and covered with dark black veins. They spiderwebbed across every inch of her skin from the roots of her blonde hair to the pads of her bare feet. Her pearlescent eyes fixed on my face, but there was no recognition there.

Oh, crap. She looks just like Jess.

I struggled to breathe.

Cami shambled to her feet and swayed from side to side.

Catching sight of her, Reed inhaled sharply. "What the—"

Cami growled and sniffed the air like an animal tracking prey. Seeming to lock in on us, she gnashed her teeth together.

The clicking noise brought me straight back to the alley the night before.

Not a prank. Not a prank.

The room spun around me as I gasped for air.

Jess had been a zombie. And now so was Cami.

Cami stumbled into the back of the couch. Seeming confused, she clawed the air in front of her, trying to reach us.

Struck dumb, all I could do was stare at what had become of my best friend.

Reed pushed me out of the way. "Ronnie."

I grabbed his arm. "Reed, no. He's... dead."

Ronnie's body twitched and spasmed on the floor.

Reed tore out of my grasp. "He's still alive." He rushed around the couch and confronted Cami. "What did you do to him?"

Cami lunged for his throat.

"Reed," I screamed.

Reed hit her with his bat.

She flew into the side of the TV stand. The ancient 36-inch tube TV wobbled and fell on top of her in a thunderous crunch of glass and bone.

Seemingly oblivious to the two-hundred-pound weight on her chest, Cami thrashed and kicked her feet.

"No, freakin' way," Reed murmured as we watched Cami try to free herself.

How can she survive being crushed by that weight?

She can't, answered an insidious voice in my head.

A rustling noise had Reed and I spinning around.

Ronnie stood at the end of the couch. The blood still pouring down his hairy chest contrasted vividly with his cadaver-white skin. Portions of his trachea were visible through the tattered flesh of his throat.

His eyes snapped open.

"Ronnie?" Reed gasped.

Ronnie's milky gaze swiveled in our direction. He let out a moan and lurched forward.

"He's one too," I shouted.

Reed shook his head as if in denial. "Get back, man. Get back." He pushed me behind him protectively.

Together we backed toward the hallway.

"We can get you help, man," Reed pleaded.

Ronnie followed us, growling and gnashing his teeth.

"Reed! Hit him."

Cursing under his breath, Reed swung his bat at Ronnie's face.

There was a wet crunch and Ronnie's brains splattered against the wood-paneled wall.

Holy crap. I'd forgotten what a hard hitter Reed was.

Ronnie slid down to the floor, the side of his head completely bashed in.

Reed dropped the bat, his entire body shaking. "I killed him. I killed him."

"No, you didn't," I said, wrapping my arms around him. "You saved us."

He pulled me against his chest, seemingly unaware that all his scars were on display.

I took a shuddering breath. *How did things go so off the rails?* Just minutes ago, I'd thought nothing could be worse than finding Reed in my bed. And now, both our best friends lay bloody on the ground.

Cami gnashed her teeth, drawing my attention back to her.

I pulled away from Reed and walked over to her. The screen had crushed her flat. Portions of her broken ribs peeked through her torn flesh. Still, she tossed her head from side to side and beat at the television set.

"Cami," I whispered, tears burning my eyes.

As she caught sight of me, her thrashing grew more frantic.

I took a step back. My brain had already accepted what my heart refused to believe. My best friend was gone, and this... mindless creature was all that remained.

She's dead.

Cami, who took me under her wing when I first started at the club. Cami, whose blasé attitude about sex never failed to shock me. Cami, who was more than a little crackpot crazy. Cami, who'd cut off her left arm for her family and me...

My legs gave out. I sank to the floor next to her.

"What is she, Lee?"

I looked up at Reed through my tears.

"I don't know."

Reed studied her with wide eyes. "She's not breathing. How can she move without breathing?"

I wiped my tears with the back of my shaking hand. "They are both dead."

Shaking his head, Reed looked at Ronnie. "I killed him."

The self-loathing in his voice had me grabbing his hand. "No. He was already dead. They're zombies." It was insane. But no other theory explained what we'd just seen. I remembered the news segment from the night before. "There have been reports of this happening to other people. We have to check the news."

"My phone is drained and..." Reed waved his hand over the smashed television. "The TV is toast."

"Eden's got a set in her room." Hoping to find some answers, I stumbled to my feet and dragged him down the hallway.

15

REED

A million conflicting thoughts and emotions assaulted me as Lee pulled me toward Eden's room. Chief among them was denial.

This isn't possible. Ronnie and Cami didn't turn into undead monsters and attack us. I didn't just splatter my best friend's brains all over the wall.

As I stumbled past Lee's room, I spied the rumpled covers on her bed. The bed she and I shared last night.

I didn't recall any details, but given the chaffing on my dick, we'd done the deed several times.

How could I forget having sex with Lee? Since puberty, it was all I'd fantasized about. What I remembered instead was a monstrous demon-looking creature standing in the back of her room.

"You're under my control," the demon had shouted in a guttural voice.

I shuddered.

Lee squeezed my hand as she pushed into Eden's room. She hadn't held my hand since we were kids, and now she was clinging to me as if she feared I'd wander off into traffic. It didn't make sense.

None of this made sense. Not me seeing a demon. Not Lee and I having sex. Not Cami and Ronnie turning into zombies.

"What a mess!" Lee exclaimed.

My gaze tripped over the dirty clothes on Eden's floor before fixing on the colorful psychedelic posters on her wall.

A wave of relief hit me. *Jesus. I get it now. I'm totally tripping.*

Ronnie must've put acid or GHB into that drink he had Aubry give me last night. It wouldn't have been the first or even the second time he'd drugged me. Just a few weeks ago, he slipped shrooms into my Subway sandwich. I'd tripped hard for the next fourteen hours.

Ronnie had laughed hysterically while recording me rolling around in the front yard screaming, "I'm the universe and the universe is me." He'd even uploaded the video to YouTube.

Fucking Ronnie.

Lee dropped my hand. "There's the TV." She pointed at the small television on Eden's cluttered desk. "Now where's the damn remote?"

I watched my flannel shirt climb her toned thighs as she searched through Eden's wrinkled pink comforter. *Damn.* I wished I could remember what happened last night. Even if it was only a hallucination, I wanted to remember every detail of the time we'd spent together.

Lee found the remote and pointed it at the TV.

Black-and-white dots danced on the screen.

Lee strode over to the TV and played with the antennas until a fuzzy image of lions resting on a grassy savanna appeared.

"Being mainly nocturnal animals, lions do most of their hunting at night," narrated a man with a crisp British accent.

Lee pounded on the remote, and the channel changed.

An image of people running out of a Chinese shopping mall appeared. It was followed by footage of people rioting in front of L.A. storefronts. The next images showed German police officers firing on a crowd gathered around a hospital. The shambling people had an all-too-familiar vacant white gaze.

It was eerily reminiscent of those zombie movies I'd binged-watched last weekend. I laughed. *Of course.* My subconscious must've cued up a zombie apocalypse trip. *Damn. Why couldn't I have hallucinated a tropical island fantasy?*

I made a sound of appreciation as I imagined Lee in a bikini.

Lee turned and gave me a questioning look before glancing back at the TV.

A tired-looking local reporter appeared on the screen. "As you can see, disturbing images are coming in from all parts of the world. Just a few hours ago, the Centers for Disease Control and Prevention along with the World Health Organization issued a joint statement alerting Americans to the discovery of a deadly new virus. This so-called Z-virus reportedly has no relation to the canine flu."

"Z-virus," I scoffed. "That's not even original."

"Shh," Lee hissed.

The screen flashed to a national press conference in Washington, where a silver-haired woman dressed in a navy suit with shoulder pads as big as her fists stood at a podium.

"At this time, we have not yet determined the origins of the Z-virus. What we do know is that it is a fatal, highly communicable, blood-borne virus. Signs of infection include the presence of dark purple or black veins that spread across the body. Current antiviral medications are proving ineffective in stopping the virus. However, our scientists are already working on a cure."

"How do you address reports that the Z-virus turns people into zombies?" shouted one of the reporters in the audience.

"Preposterous," replied the woman with a sneer. "In rare incidents, the Z-virus can cause brain damage leading to abnormal behaviors like we see with rabies."

I rolled my eyes. *Typical.* In every zombie movie, the people in charge never admitted the truth until it chewed their faces off.

Lee clenched her hands into fists. "Rabies, my ass."

Another reporter asked, "What about the purported link between the canine flu vaccination and the Z-virus?"

The woman held up her perfectly manicured hands. "Let me be clear, there's no known link between the vaccine and the Z-virus. We encourage everyone to continue receiving their vaccines. We do, however, ask that those who've already had a documented case of the canine flu hold off on getting vaccinated for now."

Lee turned to look at me. "Did you get the vaccine?"

I shook my head. *Hmm.* I thought I might have imagined a more creative origin story for the zombie apocalypse. Like maybe a genetically engineered strain of mutant mosquito or a whacked out new food additive.

She let out a relieved breath. "Good. Cami got her vaccination yesterday..."

The television screen switched back to the local reporter. "Health officials are advising residents to stay in their homes until more information becomes available. Saguaro Valley police will be enforcing curfew—"

"We have to get Eden," Lee blurted out. Her gaze flickered to the clock on Eden's nightstand. "Her arraignment starts at eight thirty. That's in fifteen minutes."

I yawned. "Have fun with that. I'm going to get some shuteye." I walked back to my room.

"What the hell?" Lee scrambled after me. "We have to get Eden."

"You get her. I'm tripping and need to sleep it off."

She grabbed my arm. "You're not tripping. This is really happening."

"Sure," I scoffed, pulling away.

She followed me into my room. "Our friends are dead."

"No. They aren't." Ronnie was probably still passed out on the living room floor with Cami. Assuming I didn't hallucinate them getting together. Actually, the more I thought about it, the more I was sure I only imagined them hooking up. No way would Cami slum it with Ronnie.

Lee shook her head, sending waves of her dark hair tumbling over her shoulders. "I don't believe this."

"That makes two of us." I sat down a little too hard on my waterbed. "If I wasn't tripping, I'd never tell you I've been in love with you for years."

She took a step back. "Reed, I—"

"I know, I know. You love me like a brother. Even my hallucination has to beat me over the head with the truth."

"This isn't a hallucination, and it isn't a joke. I thought it was a joke yesterday."

I scrubbed my face with my hands. "You expect me to believe that you let me go down on you last night." I did remember that part.

"Yes," she said, flushing.

"There's no way."

"It happened." She moved, so she was standing right in front of me. So close that I got a lungful of her sweet vanilla scent. "And you know what? I liked it. A lot. And part of me can't wait for you to do it again."

My dick turned into a rock while my mouth went dry.

"But there's another part of me that's terrified about what

that means, because I can't let myself care about you... about anyone that way."

"Why?" I asked softly.

Her eyes shadowed with memories I could only guess at.

"Is it because of what happened with your parents?"

She nodded.

"I'd never hurt you. You know that."

She rubbed her hand over her chest, drawing my gaze to the outline of her nipple pressed against the fabric.

Without thinking, I reached my hand out and cupped her breast. It sure as hell felt real.

She let out a breathy moan.

I brushed her nipple with my thumb, all the while waiting for her to knock my hand away.

She swayed toward me and then seemed to catch hold of herself. "We don't have time for this. We have to bring Eden home before it gets too bad out there."

"Mmm-hmm." I loved how flushed she'd gotten and how her breathing was hitched. At that moment, I kind of wanted to stay on that trip for the rest of my life. I tried to yank her down on the bed with me, but she resisted.

"You don't believe anything I'm saying, do you?"

I ran my hand up her thigh. "I want to. Jesus, how I want to." It was just too unrealistic. Ironically, her letting me touch her was far less believable than zombies attacking us.

She clamped her legs together, trapping my hand between them. "How about this? You help me get Eden and when we get back, we'll continue this." She motioned between the two of us.

Holy shit. Hallucination or not, I couldn't turn that down. "You're on." I jumped up and headed for the door.

"Wait, you're not even going to put a shirt on?"

I shrugged. Why bother feeling self-conscious when none of this was real? Besides, Aubry said some chicks dug scars.

Or did I hallucinate Aubry too?

Unsure, I glanced over at the bats hanging in my closet. My favorite Louisville slugger was missing from the rack.

Because I just beat Ronnie's brains out with it.

Panic clawed its way up my throat before I took a deep breath and reminded myself this was all one crazy hallucination.

Ronnie is fine. He's probably laughing his ass off at me right now. Screw him.

Maybe there was some kind of Freudian shit happening here. It was kind of cathartic to confess my love for Lee and end a toxic friendship. Maybe when I sobered up, I'd take this all to heart and start living my truth.

Lee suddenly unbuttoned my shirt.

All higher-level thinking evaporated. *Jesus.* My dick nearly tore through my jeans. "Come here." I tried to pull her over me.

"We don't have time. Here, put your shirt back on." She started to shrug off my flannel.

"You wear it," I said, thoroughly enjoying the way it looked on her. "Just leave it open like that."

She groaned. "Get your mind out of the gutter and get dressed. You can't go inside the police station half naked."

Ugh. Bossy Lee is back. I wanted sexy, surprisingly vulnerable Lee. "Can't we skip to the part where we have sex?"

"No!" she said, striding out of my bedroom. "And grab another bat for the road. We might need it."

16

LEE

Reed and I stepped outside to the sound of sirens. The banshee-like wails were quickly drowned out by the deafening sound of military helicopters tearing through the sky above.

Reed glanced up. "Cool."

"No, it's not cool." *There is some seriously bad juju going down.*

Reed's grin only widened. "This is one kick ass trip."

I thought about talking some sense into him, but quickly decided against it. There were benefits to him thinking this was all a hallucination. First, it kept him from having a complete breakdown over what happened with Ronnie and Cami. Second, it postponed the inevitable emotional fallout from us spending the night together.

I ran my suddenly damp hands down the front of my jeans. *God, I can't believe I bribed him with sex. What am I thinking?*

The answer, plain and simple, was that I wasn't thinking. I was reacting emotionally and physically, which was only going to make everything more painful later.

But there wasn't time to worry about it now. I grabbed Reed's arm. "Come on. We'll go in Cami's car." I held up the keys I'd slipped out of Cami's purse before we left. How like Cami to have a sparkly lip-shaped keychain.

Cami...

A lump rose in my throat. I took a deep breath and forced the pain away. *I can't think about her right now.*

Reed pointed the bat he was holding across the street. "We should take the love bus."

I grimaced at Gran's beat-up Volkswagen van moldering on the side of the street. Its flaking burnt-orange paint job was plastered over by hundreds of bumper stickers. "That thing hasn't run in ten years."

"I've been fixing her up." Reed flashed me a panty melting smile that made me want to drag him back into the house and screw him senseless on his waterbed. "Come on, let's take it for a spin."

How about I take you for a spin? I took a deep breath, wrangling my hormones down. "Cami's car is new." I nodded in the direction of the fire-engine red sports car.

He pursed lips that were far too kissable. "The three of us won't fit in that. Like Gran used to say, trust in the love bus." He pulled his hand from mine and danced over to the decrepit vehicle. "I'll drive. Even high I'm a better driver than you. Besides, she has a manual transmission and you can't drive stick."

True enough. Grumbling, I stuffed Cami's keys in my purse and followed him to the van.

Reed rounded the vehicle ahead of me. He opened the front passenger door and gave a gallant bow.

The smell of marijuana and cheeseburgers wafted out as I gingerly climbed into the tattered vinyl seat. It was embarrassing how tender I was down there. *Did having sex always hurt or is it something I'll get used to?* Cami would give me the unvarnished truth, but I couldn't ask her because... *she's dead.*

My insides hollowed out and tears burned the back of my eyes. I took a deep breath and let it out slowly.

By the time Reed circled back to the driver's side and jumped into the front seat, I'd forced a neutral expression on my face.

"Ready for an adventure?" He set the bat down between us.

I just stared at him, unable to deal with his jovial attitude.

He put the key in the ignition and turned. The engine coughed and made a grating metal on metal sound. "She just needs a little time to get warmed up. Don't you, love bus?" He rubbed the cracked dashboard affectionately.

I drummed my fingers on the side of the window. Time was something we didn't have. "You have one minute to get this thing started or we're switching vehicles."

"She'll start," he promised.

The engine finally turned over.

I glanced out the window as Reed drove us down the street.

The neighborhood was quiet, but that wasn't abnormal for this time of year. College students rented many of the houses on our street, and most of them went home on winter break. The rest of the homeowners weren't exactly the eight-to-five white-collar crowd.

Reed waved to Jerry, a giant bear of a man who was pushing his trash can to the curb.

Jerry, who hadn't bothered to put on a shirt, tipped his open beer in our direction.

"Gotta remember to take the trash out," Reed muttered as he made a left at the intersection.

"We've got more important things to worry about than

trash." *Like the bodies of our dead friends in the living room.* I dug my fingers into the fuzz escaping from the holes in my seat.

"Mm-hmm. So, I was thinking we could do Thai tonight."

I blinked rapidly. "What?"

"You know, for that birthday dinner you promised me. I've been craving some yellow curry from Lotus. Do you think Eden would give me a hard time if I got chicken instead of tofu? It's my birthday and all."

"Can you just drive," I said tightly.

"Right—Jesus." Reed slammed on the brakes.

Peeling myself off the dash, I scowled at him.

He was staring out at the liquor store where Uncle Duncan had parked last night. In front of the store, a man was pinned to the ground by a ragtag-looking group of men and women.

The man screamed and tried to beat them off. Flesh tore. Blood spurted.

Bile clawed its way up my throat. "Oh, my God. They're eating him alive."

"I should help that guy." Reed fumbled with his seat belt.

I grabbed his arm. "Are you crazy? There are five of them."

"Relax. I'll be fine. None of this is real." He started to open his door.

I leaned over him and yanked it closed. "Family first."

The man on the ground stopped moving. The crowd seemed to lose interest. One by one, they stood and looked our way.

"Reed, drive!"

"Aye Aye, Captain." Reed shifted, pressed the gas pedal, and the van shuddered down the street.

I glanced back at the crowd stumbling after us. The vacant looks made every hair on my body stand on end.

Reed hummed as he switched gears. "Do you want to stop at the Grinder? It's on the way?"

"We're not stopping for coffee!"

"You've got to chill. It's not as if the world is ending." Chuckling at his joke, he reached in his pocket and fished out a clove cigarette. A moment later he lit the end of it and the spicy-sweet smoke filled the van.

Where do you go when the world is ending? Away from people was the obvious answer. "We have to get out of the city." Remembering Duncan's offer made my pulse slow. *Yes. We'll go up north.* "We need to meet Uncle Duncan back at the house by nine. We're going with him to the cabin."

"That'd be fun. We could go skinny dipping in the creek like we did when we were kids. Better watch for snakes." Reed wagged his eyebrows suggestively.

The chaotic scene in front of us snared my attention. "Crap. It's a madhouse here." News vans and cars clogged the street in front of the police station.

Reed pulled up as close as he could to the entrance. "I can't park here."

"You'll have to wait for me. If they make you move, circle the block."

"But—"

I jumped out before he could argue. Clutching my purse to my side, I crossed the street.

It looked as if a press conference was going on. A gaggle of reporters with microphones outstretched surrounded a barrel-chested man in a police uniform.

"Chief Foster, what steps will the department take to control the Z-virus?"

"How is the department responding to reports of mobs attacking people throughout the city?"

"Is it true that soldiers from Fort Drexel shot three patients at the hospital earlier this morning?"

Oh, God. It sounded as if the city was going to hell in a handbasket. I hurried past the media circus to the twenty-foot-tall glass doors looming ahead. Pushing through one of the heavy doors, I came face-to-face with a metal detector and a bald officer blocking entry to the lobby.

The officer pointed at the conveyer belt. "Put your purse on the belt, ma'am."

I set my purse down and watched it move under the X-ray scanner.

He waved me forward. "Step through the metal detector, please."

I walked through.

Beep.

"I'm sorry, ma'am. Could you please step to the side and empty your pockets?"

Crap. I just remembered that I'd grabbed my father's knife and tucked it into my waistband before we'd left. Blood drained from my face. No doubt carrying a weapon into a police department was a crime.

"Ma'am."

Sweat dripped down my neck. I pulled the insides of my pockets up so he could see they were empty. "I have a belly button ring, it probably set it off." Hoping to distract him with a little flesh, I flipped up the bottom of Reed's shirt. The red gem hanging from the gold ring winked under the fluorescent light.

The officer didn't look convinced, or even mildly enticed by the sight of my abs. He grabbed a wand and waved it over my body. As the wand closed in on the small of my back, it let out a shrill noise.

"Turn around, ma'am."

With a sinking sensation in my stomach, I complied.

The officer slowly raised the hem of my shirt.

A scream inside the lobby drew his attention.

I craned my neck around to see an older man on the ground. He was spasming and flopping in a pool of blood.

The elderly woman with him cried out, "Help. My husband's hurt."

"Stay here," the officer ordered before running into the lobby.

Taking advantage of the distraction, I snatched my purse from the end of the conveyer belt and hurried after him.

A growing ring of people surrounded the man on the floor.

"What happened?"

The elderly woman wrung her hands. "I don't know. We were waiting to file a police report and Ernest collapsed."

The old man stilled. Blood continued to flow from his head.

I felt terrible for him and his hysterical wife, but there wasn't anything I could do. I sidestepped the crowd and walked up to one of the glass windows near the front of the lobby.

"I'm here to bail someone out of jail," I said to the middle-aged, curly-haired woman on the other side of the glass.

She continued staring over my shoulder at the drama unfolding behind me.

I rapped my knuckles on the glass partition to get her attention.

The woman shot me an annoyed look. "What d'ya want?"

"I'm here for Eden Walker. She was one of the protesters arrested last night."

The woman typed something into her computer. "Her hearing hasn't started yet." She jabbed her finger at the closed blue doors to my left. "Court's running behind today. Take a seat."

Chewing on my thumbnail in frustration, I walked over to

the double doors. They were locked. Through a small window in one of the doors, I could make out a hallway where a group of women wearing black-and-white striped jumpsuits stood in a long line. They were handcuffed and their feet were shackled. Several bored-looking jailers stood beside them.

I scanned the line and quickly found Eden standing over a blue-haired prisoner who was slumped against the wall. The woman's face was pale as a bone, and when Eden tried to help her to her feet, she swayed back and forth. As Eden called for one of the jailers, I got a look at the black veins running up the length of the woman's throat.

"Get away from her, Eden," I shouted through the window.

Damn it. She can't hear me.

I yanked on the door. It didn't budge.

Two paramedics, a tall thin white man and a short dark-skinned woman, rushed into the lobby.

"Get back," barked the bald officer to the growing crowd around Ernest.

People moved away, allowing the paramedics access.

"What happened?" asked the female paramedic.

The elderly woman blinked at her. "I don't know. Ernest said he wasn't feeling well, and then he keeled over."

"He hit his head pretty hard," added the officer.

The male paramedic knelt down next to Ernest and pressed his fingers against his throat. "I'm not getting a pulse."

"He's dead. Oh, my God. He should've never gotten that vaccine," screeched the older woman.

Another victim of the canine flu vaccine?

I shuddered, feeling a chill skate down my spine. *I need to get my sister out of here ASAP.*

The officer grabbed the flailing woman's arm. "Calm down, ma'am. Everything is going to be okay."

Ernest twitched and spasmed.

The male paramedic looked down at Ernest, his hand still on the injured man's neck. "What the hell? I still can't find a pulse."

Dread washed over me. I knew where this was going. "Get away from him."

Every head in the lobby swiveled in my direction.

I gulped, feeling the scrutiny of a dozen pairs of eyes. "He'll attack you. I've seen it before."

The paramedics gave me blank looks.

"What's she talking about?"

The officer took a step toward me. "Hey, didn't I tell you to wait back over there?"

Ernest made a gurgling sound. His eyes flew open.

The male paramedic leaned over him. "Relax, sir. Can you—"

Ernest clamped his jaws around the paramedic's throat.

People screamed.

"Let him go!" shouted the officer.

Ernest ripped out a hunk of the paramedic's throat.

Blood sprayed the crowd.

Ernest's wife fainted.

The paramedic collapsed on his side, his hand pressed to his neck. His eyes were wide with shock. Blood poured from his wound.

The female paramedic let out a cry and dug through her medical bag. "I've got you, Todd. Stay with me."

Horror froze me in place.

It's happening all over again.

Still gnawing on the paramedic's flesh, Ernest staggered to his feet. He stared at the surrounding people with filmy white eyes.

The officer motioned for everyone to get back. He pulled

out his gun and aimed it at the old man. "Get down on the ground."

I wanted to tell him his words were useless. Whoever Ernest had been was gone. The creature left in his place wouldn't respond to orders. But it wasn't as if the officer could've heard me over the panicked crowd.

Ernest growled and lunged for the officer.

The officer opened fire on him.

Bullets slammed into the old man's chest. Impossibly, he kept coming.

The blue doors flew open.

I jumped to the side, barely avoiding being trampled by the jailers.

They joined the officer, forming a semicircle around Ernest.

I caught the edge of the blue door before it closed and darted inside.

A sea of anxious female faces greeted me. It was clear the prisoners didn't know what was going on.

A harried-looking man in a suit stood at the front of the long hallway. "Back in line, ladies."

He was drowned out by the sound of gunfire.

"Eden," I shouted.

My sister's eyes widened when she caught sight of me. "Lee, what are you doing here?"

"Getting you out." I waved her over. "Come here."

"I can't leave Claire." She looked down at the woman who'd sunk to the floor. "She's sick and no one's helping her."

I used my no-nonsense big sister voice. "Get over here now."

"But... but..." She motioned to her shackled feet.

"Hop if you have to, but get the hell over here."

The guy in the suit looked over as she hobbled toward me. "Hey, you can't be in here."

Flipping him off, I grabbed my sister's arm and dragged her through the door into the lobby.

She started to protest, but went silent when she caught sight of the officers standing over the old man's body.

Ernest looked as though he'd been through a human-sized hole punch. He was riddled with bullet holes from his brown loafers to his bloody goatee. The top of his head had been blown off and the rest of his face was unrecognizable.

More officers streamed into the lobby from a door on the opposite side of the building.

I shoved my purse in front of Eden's hands. "Hide the cuffs under this and take short steps. Okay?"

She nodded jerkily.

Keeping a firm grip on her wrist, I tugged her forward.

We hadn't gone more than ten feet before we caught the attention of a statuesque blonde officer. "Hey, stop right there." She stepped away from the cluster of officers hovering around Ernest's body and glared in our direction.

The sound of screaming saved us.

The blonde snapped her head around and gaped at the sight of the male paramedic attacking his partner.

The female paramedic let out a cry as she tried to beat him back with her medical bag.

He clamped his jaws around her forearm and bit down.

Her scream of surprise turned into a shriek of pain.

Even from this distance, I could make out the vacant expression in the man's opaque eyes. *He's one of them.*

A sea of officers in navy blue uniforms surrounded him, guns drawn.

At the same time, a large group of reporters rushed into the building.

"Get the media out of here," shouted the blonde officer.

This is our chance. I tugged on Eden's wrist. "Keep walking."

Somehow I pulled her through the lobby and the mess of reporters.

Once through the glass doors, I forced out my anxiety in a rush of breath. We'd made it out of the station. Now our lives depended on us making it out of the city.

17

HUNTER

"**I** don't see anything," Jen said, peering down at the empty road directly below us.

I sniffed the dry air, detecting no vehicles in the vicinity.

"This could take all day," she groused. Short tendrils of dark hair danced around her face, temporarily softening her harsh features. As she scraped the errant strands back into the tight bun under her combat helmet, I couldn't help comparing the battle-hardened soldier to my mate.

They both shared the same dark hair and golden-hued skin, but that's where the similarities ended. Jen's six-foot-tall, muscular frame was closer to my hulking build than my dancer's delicate and curvaceous one. And Jen's gun-metal gray eyes were as inviting as razor blades, while Lee's soft brown eyes could seduce a eunuch.

Just thinking of my mate made my breath come faster. My night with her had been spectacular—better than I could have ever imagined. How I wished I was still lying next to her right now. Instead, she'd wake with Reed in her bed.

Jealousy left a bitter taste on my tongue. *That cocksucker better not put any moves on my mate.* It was one thing for me to claim her while in his body, it was quite another for him to touch her himself.

Jen looked down the scope of her rifle. "Do you see anything?"

"No." I stopped myself before commenting that her genetically enhanced vision was nearly as sharp as mine. Handlers never liked to be reminded that they were more closely related to us shifters than the humans they identified with.

I had no interest in pushing any more of Jen's buttons when I'd barely escaped punishment for missing her deadline. Thankfully, her eagerness to recover Dr. Hurran superseded her need to discipline me. As soon as I'd relayed the intel, she'd stopped the painful shocks to my cerebral cortex and ordered me to find a suitable location for an ambush.

It'd only taken me an hour to identify a section of isolated desert road a mile north of Javier's compound. Soon after, Jen met me on the side of the mountain.

As we'd waited behind an outcropping of sand-colored boulders, I braced myself for her interrogation. No doubt she'd want every detail of what I'd done during the time I'd been unmonitored. Surprisingly, as the minutes crawled by, she said nothing. Even stranger, she'd locked her emotions down tight.

If I concentrated hard on our bond, I picked up flickers of guilt.

What does she have to feel guilty about?

"Let's go over the plan," Jen ordered as she flicked a wayward ant that crawled across her leg. The desert combat uniform she wore blended perfectly into our sunbaked surrounding, rendering her nearly as invisible as me.

"After the vehicle hits the spike strips, I'll take out the enforcers and grab Dr. Hurran."

"I'll handle her," she corrected.

"Fine. You'll get Dr. Hurran and then we'll head back to base." We'd take the Humvee Jen had parked out of view of the road.

Jen nodded. "It'll be tricky getting through the city. Reports are it's FUBAR."

I grunted, remembering what I'd seen during my trek down here. Infected had been attacking unsuspecting humans outside urgent cares, grocery stores, and even day cares. I'd ripped an infected teacher off a toddler only to have the creature spin around and attack the child's screaming mother. My intervention had saved both the mother and child, but it was doubtful they'd survive long. They didn't have a fortified compound to shelter in like Javier.

I turned my gaze south to the Alpha's fortress. The twenty-foot walls topped with electrified barbed wire were visible in the distance. The place was locked down tighter than the army base.

Maybe I should have let Miguel take Lee there.

I immediately rejected the idea. Jen said special forces teams were currently evacuating civilians. I just had to make sure my dancer made it out of the city with them.

I cleared my throat. "I need someone evacuated."

Although she couldn't see me, Jen rolled her eyes in my direction. "Let me guess? The stripper you're obsessed with?"

When I said nothing, she scoffed. "So predictable. I'll bet that's who you ran off to screw while your scanner was being upgraded. Poor girl. Is there anything left of her?"

I stiffened. "I didn't screw her." Technically, Reed had. "I saved her from one of Javier's enforcers."

Jen shook her head as if she didn't believe me. "While your self-control was admirable, it was all for nothing. The Colonel isn't going to send a team to rescue Cherry or Lucious or whatever her name is."

"Her name is Lee." Annoyed, I made myself visible. It was taxing to cloak myself, and I needed my energy reserves for the upcoming battle.

Jen blinked as I suddenly came into view. She scanned my naked body with more interest than I was comfortable with. "What did you say?"

"My dancer goes by Lee. Although... Heaven is her first name." I waited for some sarcastic comment about stripper names, but Jen surprised me by cocking her head to the side. "Her last name isn't Walker, is it?"

"Yeah." Something moved in my periphery. I turned to see a lizard darting under the shadowy silhouette of a cactus.

Jen threw back her head and laughed until tears leaked from her eyes. "This whole fucking time... you've been obsessing after... after Lee, of all people? Oh man, that's like the definition of irony right there."

I felt as if I was missing the punchline of a joke. "How do you know Lee?" It wasn't like the Colonel allowed her kind much more freedom than they allowed us.

Her smile vanished. "That's none of your business, but you can relax. Lee and her sister are on the evacuation list."

Thank fuck. My mate's safety had been weighing heavily on my mind.

"The Colonel even assigned Dominic to pick them up, so you know they are in expert hands."

My relief morphed into anger. "So, the fucker is out now."

Jen gave me a wary look. "I know you're pissed at him, but you need to let it go."

Pissed? She had no fucking idea. "How can you defend him after what he did?" When she said nothing, I went for her heart. "He doesn't love you. You know he was willing to take a demotion to avoid the Colonel's order to marry you, right?"

Although her expression didn't change, sadness thrummed through our bond.

I immediately felt like the biggest piece of shit. "Sorry."

She set her jaw and looked up at the hawk turning lazy circles in the bright blue sky above us. "Love isn't something we can control. Life would be so much easier if it were."

I shifted uncomfortably, not knowing how to respond. Jen and I had never been close, not like me and Dom had been back before he'd betrayed me.

As if reading my mind, Jen said, "Dominic may not love me, but he sure as hell cares for you."

I recoiled at her words. "The fuck he does."

She gave me a ghost of a smile. "The first thing he asked for when he got out was you."

I bared my teeth. "I can't wait for our reunion." *I'm going to tear that motherfucker's head off.*

Guilt pulsed through our bond again. "Hunter, the Colonel is making Dominic your—" The sound of car engines interrupted her.

We both cranked our heads around to see a convoy of black Mercedes approaching.

Jen cursed. "You said there would be four or five enforcers."

"Luis said there'd be four or five in her escort," I replied. "I'd assumed that meant enforcers."

"You know what they say about assumptions."

I scoffed. "Doesn't matter how many they have." *I'd kill them all.*

Down below, the first Mercedes drove across the spike strip. All four tires blew, causing it to veer into the next lane. Flapping rubber could be heard as it coasted to a stop.

The vehicle directly behind it swerved to avoid the strip and crashed into the guardrail.

The third vehicle screeched to a stop and was rear-ended by the last vehicle that couldn't slow in time.

The smell of burning rubber scorched my nose as car

doors flew open and nearly a dozen enforcers swarmed protectively around the second vehicle.

Jen stated the obvious. "Dr. Hurran must be in that car."

"Give me your orders." I crouched down, bloodlust stirring inside me.

Jen took a deep breath as if considering her words carefully. "Hunter, neutralize any entity that interferes or might interfere with our current mission. This order supersedes all other orders."

My beast let out a roar of delight as I shifted. Bones and joints popped. Sinew and muscles realigned. A second later, I rose as a monstrous creature that towered over my handler and the enforcers below.

Jen slapped my flank. "Go get 'em."

Snarling, I leapt from our mountain perch directly onto the roof of the third Mercedes. The shiny black metal crumpled under my tremendous weight.

Jen, who'd jumped down onto the road, shook her head. "Always have to make a grand entrance, don't you?"

If I could have communicated with her in this form, I would have answered, "Hell, yeah."

The black-clad enforcers fired on us. Their bullets ricocheted off my hide.

Jen ducked behind the flattened vehicle as I sauntered toward our enemies.

My beast urged me to tear through them, but there was no fun in that. I slowed my pace, letting them get a good look at death approaching.

The largest enforcer, the one I recognized as Santiago, Javier's Head Enforcer, was the first to throw his useless weapon to the ground. He barked an order in Spanish, then ripped off his clothes and shifted.

The other males followed his lead, and soon a group of snarling black leopards were circling me.

I chuffed in amusement at their show of aggression.

Santiago lunged for my throat.

A swipe of my paw sent him flying over Jen's head. His feline body hit the asphalt with a wet crunch.

"Stop playing around and kill them," she ordered. She turned and fired a bullet into Santiago's skull before he could heal his injuries. Then she ran toward the second vehicle.

Hissing, the leopards turned toward her.

Unable to allow any threat to my handler, I attacked in a blur of claws and fangs. Moments later, the pavement was wet with blood and not a single leopard drew breath. Shaking viscera from my shaggy mane, I let out a triumphant roar.

"Be still, beast," shouted an all too familiar voice.

I looked up to see Javier exiting his smashed Mercedes. Oddly enough, he didn't look angry that I'd killed his enforcers or fearful that he'd be next.

My surprise at seeing him gave way to burning rage. For weeks I'd wanted to punish the Alpha for coveting my dancer. *Time to teach that fucker who's really in charge.* I prepared to attack, but every muscle in my body locked up. *Shit! He is more powerful than I am.* Panicked, I searched for Jen. Surely, her commands could override his.

A wave of dizzying pain suddenly rushed through our bond.

Jen!

I found her at the other end of the car, writhing at the feet of Dr. Hurran.

There was no mistaking the dusky-skinned scientist holding a cattle prod over my handler. Dr. Hurran was even wearing the same white lab coat she always wore.

Jen made a garbled sound.

"Quiet," ordered Dr. Hurran, repeatedly shocking Jen with the high voltage device.

Jen's entire body seized up. Another burst of pain exploded through our bond.

I snarled, furious I could do nothing to help her.

Javier made a tsking sound as he watched my handler shake and thrash in the dirt. "I thought Titan soldiers were powerful."

Dr. Hurran sniffed. "They are. But we microchip them too. And when their chip is exposed to high voltage..." She brought the cattle prod down on Jen again.

Jen's body contorted so violently, her spine snapped with a loud crack.

Dr. Hurran let out a cold laugh.

Jen's torment thrummed through our link. I shifted back to my human form so I could shout, "Stop hurting her!"

Javier's amber gaze swung back to me. "The beast is protective of her."

"She's his handler. It's part of his programming to follow her orders and protect her as if she was his alpha," Dr. Hurran explained.

"Interesting," Javier said, rubbing his chin thoughtfully. "Can you reprogram it?"

The scientist tossed her head back arrogantly. "Of course."

Javier smiled. "And you say it can become invisible?"

"For short periods of time," Dr. Hurran confirmed. "He's also venomous."

Javier's grin widened. "And it looked fast?"

"We've clocked him at 300 miles per hour."

"Magnífico!" Javier rubbed his hands, looking like a giddy child. "What is it? You must tell me."

My breath caught in my throat. I too had wondered at my origins. I'd always assumed my kind was some sort of monstrous wolf and feline shifter hybrid.

"Vulcari."

"Vulcari?" Javier echoed, drawing out the unfamiliar word.

"The species is not of this realm." Dr. Hurran gave him a smug grin.

What the fuck did that mean?

Javier let out an audible gasp. "So, it is true then?"

I glanced between them. *What's true?*

Dr. Hurran nodded.

Javier eyed me with wonder. "Please tell me there are more like it."

Dr. Hurran shook her head. "Unfortunately, all the Typhos subjects were terminated except this one and his twin."

My heart skipped a beat. *Ghost is alive?* The roaring in my ears drowned out the rest of their conversation. "Where is my brother?" I demanded. *How did I not know he was alive?*

"*Silencio*," commanded Javier. But he turned to Dr. Hurran and asked her the same question.

The scientist shrugged. "Dr. Zimmerman moved him to an undisclosed research facility."

"No matter. We'll find him, won't we?" He and Dr. Hurran exchanged some private joke.

Jen opened her blood-rimmed eyes. "Hunter," she whispered. "I order you... to run straight to Dominic..."

I growled under my breath. I wouldn't have left her even if I could have moved.

"I-ignore all other orders. Go to Dominic now," Jen wheezed.

Suddenly, I was free to move. I snarled at Javier, wanting more than anything to destroy him and that traitor scientist, but I couldn't fight Jen's orders.

"Come back!" Javier shouted as I turned and ran. The power in his voice made my head ring, but it wasn't enough to counter my handler's order.

I heard Dr. Hurran shout, "Kill his handler."

A gun fired.

The bond between Jen and I flared with agonizing pain and then snapped. Static burst through my inner ear and all my sense of Jen's emotions vanished.

She's dead. My handler was dead.

Instead of feeling relief that I was finally free of her oversight, an unexpected wave of grief hit me.

Jen had been decent to me. She didn't deserve to die.

It was yet another nail in Javier's coffin. Soon he and Dr. Hurran would die by my hands. But they'd have to get in line because right now I had someone else to kill.

Jen's last order was the greatest parting gift she could have given me. I was going to do as she ordered. I'd run straight to Dominic, and then I'd send the bastard straight to hell.

18

LEE

I'd never been more excited to see Gran's stupid bus than when I spied it parked behind one of the news vans.

I waved at Reed and dragged Eden over to the vehicle. "Come on."

She stumbled after me. "Lee, you could go to prison for this."

"Just get in." I slid open the back door, revealing two raggedy bench seats facing one another.

She stuck out her chin the way she always did when she was about to pitch a fit. "This is insane."

I tightened my grip on her arm. "Don't make me throw you in."

Reed twisted around. "Hey, Eden. Everyone's turning into zombies. Cool, huh?"

Eden looked between us. "Are you high?"

"Totally." Reed laughed. "I'm tripping hard."

Two police cars, lights flashing and sirens blaring, pulled in behind us.

A rush of adrenaline had me shoving my sister into the

van. I clambered in behind her and slammed the door. "Go," I shouted to Reed.

He shifted, and the van slowly puttered forward. He shifted again, and the van reversed a few inches.

I could feel the vein in my temple throbbing. "Get this hunk of junk moving."

"Patience, woman. We're boxed in."

I pushed the dirty curtain out of the way and peeked through the window. Thankfully, the officers were running toward the station. My blood pressure fell a couple of notches.

Reed flipped a U-turn and drove us back the way we came.

Letting out a deep breath, I sat down next to my sister and met her incredulous stare. "Don't give me that look. You're the one that screwed up." I pursed my lips and thinned my voice. "Sissy, I promise no more protests. I'm just going to have coffee with friends tonight." I finished my impersonation of her by flipping back my hair.

She paled. "I can explain—"

I held up my hand. "I'm tired of excuses. Reed, step on it." Hopefully, we could still make it home in time to meet Uncle Duncan and get the hell out of town. If we didn't...

I swallowed hard. *No. Not thinking about that.*

Eden jangled her cuffs. "How am I going to get out of these?"

"We'll find some bolt cutters." I'd bet my fluffy angel wings that Uncle Duncan had a pair. He was usually prepared for anything.

Eden touched her neck. Her eyes widened. "Sasha's collar. The police impounded it." She glanced behind us. "We have to go back."

"The hell we will. You can get another collar, okay?" I got that Eden was mourning the loss of her dog. Hell, I missed the pit bull mix too. But her collar wasn't worth getting arrested over.

She jerked her head up. "You just don't get it, do you? I wear Sasha's collar to remember her and the senseless reason for her death. I went to jail protesting her killers and their murderous laws, and I won't stop fighting them no matter—"

"Can it, Edie," I said with an eye roll. "We've got bigger problems than Order 1537. People are turning into monsters. That prisoner next to you in line was infected with the Z-virus."

"What are you talking about?"

"I'm talking about the blue-haired chick. Cami had those same black veins before she attacked Ronnie."

Eden blinked. "I'm not following. What happened to Ronnie?"

Reed stopped the van at a light and glanced back at her. "I beat Ronnie's head in with a bat this morning."

"He was a zombie," I clarified.

"I also took out Cami," Reed said, sounding a bit too happy about it.

Eden made a choking sound.

"Don't freak. None of this is real." Reed waved his hands around.

"It's real," I said with a sigh.

Eden shook her head. "You've both completely lost it."

"We did lose it," Reed said, giving her a meaningful look in the rear-view mirror. "Lee and me. Last night."

"Reed!" I didn't want Eden to know about that. Ever.

"You two had sex?" she shrieked. Her eyes went so wide I was afraid they would pop out of her skull. She turned her gaze toward me, no doubt waiting for me to contradict him.

I looked away, my face heating.

"Well, it's about damn time."

"What?" That wasn't the reaction I'd expected.

She laughed. "The sexual tension between you two was getting ridiculous."

That was news to me. "What do you mean—"

The van shuddered, and the engine died.

"What the hell!" I glanced out the windshield. My blood chilled when I saw we were stopped near the corner liquor store again. "Reed, get the van moving."

"Working on it."

"What's going on over there?" Eden tapped on the glass.

I pushed her out of the way to look through the side window. Across the street, a dozen people shuffled around the empty parking lot shared by Eros and the sex shop.

It took me two seconds to recognize Jess in the crowd. A large bald man lurched beside her. He was missing his left arm.

"Oh, my God. That's Max." I struggled to breathe. My boss was a zombie too.

A bloody hand slammed against the front passenger window.

"What is that?" screeched Eden.

There was no mistaking the lime-green bowling shirt. "Cal," I said, staring at the remains of the sex shop owner in horror.

Hunks of flesh were gouged from his face. One eye was missing and the other dangled from the socket.

Guilt swamped me. If I hadn't asked for his help last night, would he still be alive?

The glass cracked.

"Reed!" I shouted.

Reed tried turning the ignition over again. The van engine made a grinding noise.

No. This can't be happening.

The front passenger window shattered. Cal reached inside.

"Okay, okay." Reed's way too calm words were punctuated by the sound of him twisting the ignition and pounding his foot on the pedals.

Cal clawed in Reed's direction.

"Back off, man." Reed said, trying to avoid Cal's outstretched hands.

"More are coming," Eden shrieked.

Dread filled me as I shot another look out the side window.

The sight of the zombie horde lumbering across the street made my knees shake.

Jess was at the head of the pack, her intestines swaying in front of her like macabre tentacles.

I drew the knife from my waistband with shaking hands. Running wasn't an option with Eden in shackles. "Reed!"

He turned the ignition one more time, and the engine warbled to life. We pulled away just as Jess and her zombie crew reached the back of the van.

Thank God.

My relief was short-lived.

Cal clung to the door, his skinny legs dragging on the street.

"Goddamn it." I sprang from my seat and moved into the front of the van. "Let go," I shouted, stabbing at his spindly arms. Any sympathy I had for the man evaporated when he gnashed his teeth at me.

"Stab him in the head," Reed yelled. "You have to take out their brain."

I leaned across the seat and tried to stab Cal in his empty eye socket.

The van jerked to the left as Reed swerved to avoid a child-sized figure lurching across the street. "Kid zombies. Now that's just wrong," he muttered.

I nicked Cal's ear.

He snapped at me. His fetid breath scorched the hair on my arm as I barely pulled away in time.

Shrieking, I dropped my knife onto the seat.

"Move out of the way," Reed shouted, grabbing his bat.

I moved back as Reed leaned over.

Keeping one hand on the steering wheel, he swung the bat at Cal.

Crunch. The side of Cal's head crumpled in, like an egg that had been squeezed too hard. He went limp and disappeared over the side of the van.

Reed settled back in his seat, bloody bat draped over his lap. "That was fun."

All I could do was stare at him. "Who are you, and what did you do with my friend Reed?"

He gave me one of his infuriating grins. "This is my hallucination, right? I get to save my woman from the monsters."

At some point, I really was going to have to bitch slap him into reality.

I glanced back at Eden.

She was hyperventilating.

At least she understood the gravity of what was happening. "Breathe, Eden. Just breathe."

She nodded, her fingers digging into her jumpsuit-covered thighs.

I shoved my knife back into my waistband and sat down in the glass-covered front passenger seat.

Eden let out a shaky breath. Her handcuffs jingled as she pushed her hair out of her face. "What the hell is going on?"

I rubbed the side of my head, feeling a stress headache coming on. "All we know is that people are dying and coming back as zombies. It seems to have something to do with the canine flu vaccine."

She reached for her throat again. When her fingers found

the bare skin of her neck instead of Sasha's collar, they fluttered to her lap. "What are we going to do?"

"We're going with Uncle Duncan to the mountains." If we'd missed his visit to the house, we'd still head up north. But we'd definitely squish ourselves in Cami's car. I was done with this death trap.

Reed turned the van down our street and whistled. "Did Uncle Duncan get a black Mercedes?"

"No, why?"

My question was answered when Reed pulled the van up to the sidewalk and two men in dark suits stepped out of the luxury car parked in our driveway.

The shorter of the two men looked in our direction and grinned. Sunshine glinted off his gold front teeth.

Nero.

I shuddered, a pit forming in my stomach.

What is Javier's man doing at our house?

"Stay here," I ordered Reed and Eden. "I know these guys. They're bad news." Ignoring their questioning looks, I opened the van door and stepped out.

Nero's grin widened as I approached. "*Hola, señorita.* We've been waiting for you."

I stopped in the middle of the lawn, a few feet from the gravel driveway. My gaze bounced between Nero and the six-and-a-half-foot tall man with him.

"I'm Nero and this is Carlos." Nero said, motioning at the muscular man. The action opened his suit jacket just enough to reveal the handgun holstered at his hip.

"Why?" I hated the waver in my voice.

"*Señor* Diaz is inviting you to stay with him." Nero's smile failed to reach his eyes. The darkness in them made me want to run back to the van.

"N-no, thanks," I stuttered.

"The city is too dangerous now. *Señor* Diaz will keep you safe." His tone held a hard edge.

I took several steps back. "I'll be fine here with my family."

"They are welcome too. Carlos, bring them."

Carlos strode over to the van.

"Leave them alone," I shouted.

Nero raised a hand to stop me from following Carlos. He put his other hand on his weapon. "We can do this the easy way, or the hard way."

I swallowed hard. My mind spun as I remembered all the horrific things I'd heard about Javier's gang.

A moment later, Carlos returned with Reed and Eden in tow. He walked them past me, stopping only when he reached the Mercedes.

Reed looked excited. "Now I'm hallucinating gangsters! Sweet!"

Eden, looking much less thrilled, stumbled behind them in her shackles.

"Who is this? A sister?" Nero's grin widened and his snakeskin boots crunched in the gravel as he walked down the driveway. When he reached Eden, he stroked a finger down her cheek. "You're almost as pretty as your sister, jailbird."

I clenched my hands into fists. "Get away from her."

Nero's smile faded. He walked back toward me. The menacing expression on his face matched the deadly gleam in his eye. "You will speak to me with respect."

"Fuck you."

Faster than a striking cobra, Nero backhanded me.

"Lee!" Reed struggled to get out of Carlos's grip.

Holding my stinging cheek, I glared at Nero. "We're not going anywhere with you."

Nero raised his hand as if to strike me again.

"Don't touch her." Yanking away from Carlos, Reed charged Nero and tackled him to the ground. He got in two or three good punches before Carlos rushed over and slammed his fist into the side of Reed's head.

Reed tumbled off Nero and landed on his back, a dazed look on his face.

"Stop!" I screamed as Carlos repeatedly kicked Reed in the head.

I pulled my knife and jumped on the big man's back. Before I could stab him, Nero ripped me off Carlos and flung me into the grass. My knife flew out of my hand.

"Fucking bitch," Nero spat down at me. He stepped around his partner and pulled out a gun.

All the oxygen rushed out of my lungs as Reed's death flashed before my eyes. "Don't shoot him. I'll do whatever you want."

"No—" Reed started to say before Nero pistol-whipped him across the face so hard he sprawled out on the driveway, unconscious.

Nero pressed his gun against Reed's forehead. "I've changed my mind. Only the girls are invited."

Panic choked me. "Please don't shoot him."

Carlos grabbed a handful of my hair and yanked me to my knees. "Get up and get into the car."

A familiar voice interjected. "Let her go, son."

We all turned to see my uncle limping up the driveway. His revolver was drawn and pointed at Carlos's head. "Put your hands up. Now."

Carlos released my hair and put his hands up.

The knot in my chest loosened. *Everything's going to be okay.* I grabbed my knife and got to my feet.

Uncle Duncan took the huge man's sidearm and handed it to Eden who'd been frozen like a statue this entire time. My uncle then shoved Carlos toward the Mercedes. "Now *you* get into the car."

With a quick glance at Nero, Carlos slid into the driver's seat.

Nero laughed. "And here I thought picking up the stripper was going to be boring."

"It's time for you to leave, son." Uncle Duncan slowly ambled to Reed's side. He looked down at Reed's bleeding face and frowned.

"Don't call me son." Nero aimed his gun at my uncle.

Eden pointed the gun she was holding at Nero. "Drop your gun or I'll shoot."

Nero glanced back at her. "Shoot then, little jailbird."

Eden's hands shook so hard, her handcuffs rattled. "I'll do it. I swear."

Nero made a dismissive sound.

Uncle Duncan straightened his shoulders. "Look, son. I've already called the cops. I'd suggest y'all get moving before they get here."

"Fine, we'll go. But not without you, *señorita*." Nero walked over and grabbed my arm.

"Go to hell." I sliced him across the face with my knife and ran toward Reed and my uncle.

The sound of a gun safety clicking off had me spinning back around.

❧ 19 ❧
LEE

The gangster pointed his gun at my head. "No one marks Nero Benitez," he shouted as he pulled the trigger.

Crack.

Something heavy crashed into my side, pushing me to the ground. Ears ringing, I looked up in confusion.

My uncle stood where I'd been, a crimson stain blooming across the front of his favorite denim shirt.

"No!" I cried. He'd taken the bullet meant for me.

"Uncle Duncan!" Eden shrieked.

He gave her a sad smile and collapsed.

I scrambled over to his side. "I'm so sorry." Hot tears ran down my face as I pressed my hands to his chest, trying to stop the bleeding.

My uncle opened his mouth as if to say something, but all that came out was a spurt of blood that stained his silver mustache red.

The sounds of moaning and clicking filled the air. Zombies were close. A lot of them. That should've filled me with terror, but all I could think about was the man dying in front of me.

Carlos started the car and rolled down the window. "Nero. The dead are coming. We need to go."

Something warm and metallic pressed against my head.

"I'll give *Señor* Diaz your regards, bitch."

I glared at the asshole pressing a gun against my head. Nero hurt Reed and shot my uncle. *He deserves to die.* Letting out a battle cry, I knocked the gun out of his hand, picked up Uncle Duncan's revolver, pointed it at Nero's face, and pulled the trigger.

Bang.

The side of Nero's head exploded.

The car door flew open. Carlos jumped out and rushed toward me.

Bang. Bang. Bang.

He crashed to the ground like a fallen tree.

Eden stood behind him, a smoking gun in her shaking hands.

Stunned, I blinked at my sister. I'd never thought her capable of murder.

"Good girls," Uncle Duncan wheezed. His eyelids fluttered shut and he let out his last breath.

He's gone.

A scream boiled up inside me. I wanted to shout out the unfairness of his death. And all the deaths of the people I'd loved. But screaming wouldn't bring them back.

"Sissy." Eden hopped over. "A bunch of those things are coming. What do we do?"

I wiped away my tears with the back of my hand and shoved Uncle Duncan's gun into my waistband. Then I picked up my knife and Nero's gun.

Either we barricaded ourselves in the house or drove one of the cars out of here. I looked down at Reed's bloody face and made a split-second decision. "Help me get him into the house."

While Eden and I struggled to drag Reed up the driveway, the spine-tingling sound of clicking teeth grew in volume.

Unable to help myself, I glanced down the street. The size of the horde lumbering toward us stole my breath. Movement out of my peripheral vision had me glancing in the opposite direction.

Jerry, still shirtless, lumbered across his yard. He must've been coming to investigate the gunshots.

I had to warn him. "Jerry, get back inside your house."

Jerry canted his head in my direction. The blood streaming from the tattered skin of his neck looked like a crimson scarf in the bright light.

Crap. He's one of them.

Letting out a garbled noise, he shambled toward us.

There was a crashing noise. Mrs. Munoz from two doors down stumbled out her front windows. She was saturated in so much blood it looked as if she'd bathed in it.

Seeing us, she lifted her head and moaned. The blood-chilling sound was echoed by her two children, who appeared behind her.

Oh, God. Everyone's turning into monsters.

"Lee!" Eden gasped. "We have to hurry!"

Grunting, we dragged Reed through the lawn littered with red plastic cups.

As we pulled him up the front step, a hysterical laugh bubbled from my lips. Just hours ago, my biggest worry was who'd clean up the mess from the party. Now, I didn't know if we'd survive the day.

Eden wrenched opened the unlocked door and together we dragged Reed into the house.

As soon as we were all in, Eden slammed the door closed and turned the dead bolt.

As if that will keep them out.

I swung my gaze around the living room, realizing we had the same floor-to-ceiling windows Mrs. Munoz had just crashed through. "We need to cover the windows."

Eden ran to the entryway closet, opened the door, and rummaged through it.

"What the hell are you doing?"

She held up an old collar of Sasha's. "I need this." She buckled it around her neck.

"Seriously? If the zombies don't kill you, I will. Go grab the other side of the couch."

Eden took two steps forward and froze. She'd caught sight of Cami writhing under the television set.

"Eden."

She jerked her head up. "What?"

I pointed at the couch. "Help me push this to the window."

"Right." She hobbled over and then gasped when she saw Ronnie's body lying on the floor.

I smacked her arm. "Focus."

The sounds of clicking and moaning were getting louder. The zombies had to be right outside.

"Okay," she said in a shaky voice. "Let's do this."

Between the two of us, we managed to push the couch against the largest window and flip it over so it blocked most of the glass.

"Do the same thing with the other furniture," I shouted as hands slammed against the windows.

I grabbed the recliner and dragged it in front of an open window while Eden moved one of the big speakers against another window.

Glass shattered.

"They're coming through," Eden shrieked, her eyes wild.

We backed away from the windows.

Bloody arms and legs pushed their way inside.

"Shoot them," I screamed, raising Nero's gun.

Eden raised Carlos's gun and fired on the first zombie, who pushed his way past the couch.

It was Jerry.

"The head. Aim for the head," I cried, remembering Reed's advice. I glanced over at his unconscious body lying in the hallway.

We have to protect him.

Eden's next shot took off the top of Jerry's skull.

He went down and stayed down.

Mrs. Munoz and her kids stumbled over the recliner.

Eden stepped forward, but then lowered her gun.

"Eden, shoot!"

"I can't. They're kids," she cried.

"They're monsters."

Her hands shook. The gun wavered in the air.

Crap. "Get back." I pushed her behind me and unloaded into our neighbor and her ten- and thirteen-year-old boys. The kids were faster and harder to hit than the adults. I emptied the handgun before they finally hit the floor.

I threw down Nero's empty gun and drew Duncan's revolver.

"I'm out of ammo. What do we do?" Eden screamed.

"Take this, protect Reed." I gave her my knife and pushed her toward the hallway.

I continued firing on the zombies, but as soon as one collapsed, another creature seemed to take its place.

The living room soon filled with them. Some had black veins mottling their faces and skin. Others had horrific wounds to their necks and torsos. All of them clicked their teeth excitedly as their frosted gazes fixed on us.

I stumbled back toward Eden and Reed. *How can we possibly survive this?*

We could barricade ourselves into one of the rooms, but how long before the zombies broke through? *Minutes? Seconds?*

The sound of rapid gunfire made me jump.

"Machine guns," Eden gasped, a startled expression on her face.

While my mind struggled to process what that might mean, the front door crashed open.

A dark-haired giant wearing military fatigues and a tactical vest covered in knives stormed into the house. He turned to face the zombies and, in movements so quick they barely registered, threw a succession of knives at the creatures.

Every single one fell to the floor, a knife embedded in their forehead.

"Wow," Eden said under her breath as she watched him retrieve his knives from the corpses.

Wow is right.

Not only did he have perfect, deadly aim, the man was gorgeous. His bulging muscles, chiseled cheekbones, and full lips made my heart pound harder. I nearly swooned when he turned his attention to us huddled in the hallway. "Are you okay?"

Eden and I nodded in unison.

"Have any of you been bitten?"

We shook our heads.

A tall, muscular, dark-skinned woman also decked out in camo prowled into the house. She pointed her assault rifle at the bodies on the floor. Seemingly satisfied there was no threat, she turned to the man. "Sarge, I've eliminated the infected outside the house, but more will come."

With a grunt, he looked down at her. "The list?"

The female soldier reached into her pocket and handed him a piece of paper.

He looked at it for a second, then pinned us with his black gaze. "Is Eden Walker or H. Lee Walker here?"

"Yes," I said, my voice coming out as a squeak. I cleared my throat. "I'm Lee and this is my sister Eden."

"Good." He folded the paper and handed it back to the woman. "I'm Sergeant Dominic Rosario with the U.S. Army, and this is Corporal Darcy Ross. We're evacuating civilians from the Valley. Come with us."

Hope pulsed to life inside me. *We're being rescued.*

I pointed at Reed. "Our roommate is with us too. He's hurt, but he hasn't been bitten."

The sergeant's expression tightened. "He's not on the list. He stays."

I reared back. "No. He comes with us."

"My orders are clear, Ms. Walker. Only those on the list come with us."

I met the sergeant's scowl with one of my own. "Screw your list. Either Reed comes with us, or we stay."

We'll take Uncle Duncan's truck and get the hell out of town.

Darcy let out a huff of air. "Ungrateful civvies. We should leave 'em, Sarge."

The sergeant took a step closer to me. "If you don't come with me right now, you'll be dead within twenty-four hours."

Cobbling together my last bit of strength, I lifted the revolver to show him I was armed. He didn't need to know I was out of ammo. "I might surprise you."

His gaze swept over me. His lips quirked up. "I think you might."

I straightened my spine, not liking the way my body warmed under his gaze. "Reed is coming with us."

He sighed and motioned us toward the door. "Fine. We're burning daylight."

"I'll get, Goldilocks," the female soldier said, throwing Reed over her shoulder and marching out the door.

My jaw dropped. It'd taken all my sister's and my strength

to drag Reed inside and Darcy had deadlifted him with one arm.

"Be careful. He has a head injury," Eden called out, running after the super soldier.

Super soldiers. Zombie hordes. Gangsters. It was too much. Feeling dizzy, I stumbled over a corpse.

Moving in a blur, the sergeant caught me and hauled me against his chest. "Are you always this much trouble, Ms. Walker?"

The heat of his skin sent tiny electric shocks down my body. Gasping for breath, I gazed into his dark eyes. Something indefinable passed between us and, for a moment, I was hit with the strangest feeling that I belonged to this man.

I immediately rejected the ridiculous idea. I'd never belong to any man. Not Javier. Not Reed. And certainly not this guy.

Lifting my chin, I countered, "Are you always this much of a pain in the ass, Sergeant Rosario?"

The sergeant stared at me as if I'd whacked him with a two-by-four. Then he let out a deep rumbling laugh and carried me outside.

HUNTER

Reaching the city limits, I cloaked myself and began the hunt for my former master. I tried to ignore the static crackling inside my ears. It was an ever-present reminder that Jen was gone. Our bond was broken and the chaos that wrought on my mind and body threatened to overwhelm me.

To keep from losing it, I focused on how I was going to kill Dom. I'd creep up to him while he was unaware and whisper my brothers' names into his ear. He'd spin around, and I'd show no mercy as I ripped off every one of his limbs. When he was a shrieking stump on the ground, I'd devour him alive.

My dark plans faded as I made it deeper into the city. Everywhere I looked humans were being attacked. Their screams rang in my ears and the smell of their blood singed my nostrils. Mobs of dead ambushed them in the blood-soaked streets—ripping them from cars or crashing through building windows to get them. After all the pain humans had inflicted on me throughout my life, I thought I'd be unmoved by their slaughter. I'd thought wrong.

Dom's scent led me to an all too familiar street. The knot in my stomach tightened as I surveyed my mate's neighborhood. It was unrecognizable from the night before. Fences were trampled, windows were shattered, and flies swarmed several male carcasses lying in the street.

It would have taken an enormous horde to do this kind of damage. An unfamiliar emotion gripped me. *What if Lee didn't survive?*

Forcing back panic, I ran faster. The first thing I saw as I rounded the turn to Lee's house were dozens of corpses covering nearly every inch of her yard and driveway. I took a deep inhale, relieved as fuck to find my mate's scent emanating from inside her house and not from the piles of dead.

My relief grew as I spied an armored transport vehicle idling next to the sidewalk.

Dom's here.

The acrid scent of gunpowder and the slew of brass casings scattered between corpses told me he wasn't alone. Dom only used guns as a last resort.

Just as I was trying to determine who he was traveling with, a familiar female soldier emerged from Lee's house. Darcy, a close friend of Jen's, was carrying Reed's unconscious body over her shoulder.

"Be careful. He could have a concussion," Lee's younger sister cried as she hopped behind Darcy in a striped jumpsuit and shackles.

Seeing Lee's loved ones relatively unharmed gave me hope. I charged toward the smashed in door and nearly collided with Dom carrying Lee out of the house.

After registering that my mate was alive, I jumped out of their path.

Dom stopped. Then with some kind of uncanny awareness, stared in my direction.

The granite-faced bastard looked a little leaner and meaner than the last time I'd seen him. But prison would do that to a male. Based on his clean tactical uniform, he hadn't seen much action.

Lee, on the other hand, looked as if she'd gone through hell and back. "Where are you taking us, Sergeant?" she asked, pushing a clump of blood-soaked hair out of her face.

Alarm arrowed through me as I sniffed the air around her. Thankfully, I detected no injury. The blood belonged to others.

"To our RP," Dom responded.

Lee angled her head to look up at him. "What?"

"It's short for rally point. A Chinook will meet us there."

"A Chinook?" she echoed.

"A transport helicopter," he explained.

She crinkled her nose adorably. "Can you talk without the military lingo?"

"Where's the fun in that?" he quipped.

I stared at Dom in shock. *Did the bastard just smile?* I could count on one hand the number of times I'd seen him express happiness, and they'd all been after he took out a target with a particularly good knife throw.

Lee tried to squirm out of his hold. "I can walk."

Dom tightened his arms around her. "You weren't doing a great job back there."

What the fuck? Dom never coddled anyone... ever.

"Well, excuse me." Lee lifted her chin. "I've just faced off with a bunch of gang members who killed my uncle..." She swallowed hard. "... and then had to deal with my zombie neighbors."

The brittleness of her voice gutted me. *I should have been here to protect her.*

Dom's gaze softened. "Sounds like you've had a morning."

I'd never seen him look at anyone with that kind of warmth. Not me. Not his soldiers. Not even his wife.

The reminder of Jen's fate made my throat ache.

Lee glanced over Dom's shoulder at the driveway. "Can I bring my uncle's body back with us?"

"No."

"But I need to bury him."

"That won't be possible." Dom's expression turned to stone.

She wasted her breath arguing with him while he brought her to the transport vehicle and set her down next to her sister and Reed.

"Hostiles inbound," Darcy shouted, bringing my attention and Dom's to the lurching figures at the end of the street.

"Let's move out," Dom ordered.

As I stared at the back of his close-cropped hair, I debated my next move. Jen was dead, and I'd successfully completed her last order. That made me free. Free to search for my brother. Free to take my mate somewhere safe where we could start a life together. Free to avenge the genocide of my family.

Yeah, let's start with that. A simmering rage churned inside me as I slowly crept up behind Dom.

He paused in the middle of opening the vehicle door and spun around. "Enough with your games, Hunter. Where's Sergeant Brooks?"

I made myself visible. "Dead. Like you're about to be." With a snarl, I extended my claws and raised them over his head.

Dom spun around.

The moment I met his icy black gaze, unwanted memories slammed into me. Years of training missions, covert operations, and battles we'd fought together flashed in my mind. We'd been the deadliest handler-beast team in military history. Over the years, our working relationship had developed into mutual respect, then friendship, if such a thing was even possible between our kind. It's what made his betrayal that sweltering morning three years ago even more gut-wrenching.

Like a flash, he yanked up his sleeve and tapped the device grafted onto his forearm. "Activate handler pairing."

The connection snapped between us so quickly there was no time to react. Unlike my link to Jen, which had been thin and narrow, this bond was vast and all-encompassing. It felt as if titanium steel cables, forged in blood and war, now anchored me to him.

I howled in fury, trying to fight the recalibration of my body and mind. But it was impossible. In a flash of clarity, I realized I hadn't been left unmonitored earlier because of any scanner upgrades. It'd been because they were preparing to re-pair me to Dom. *Fuck.* Jen knew. *This must've been the reason for her guilt back in the desert.*

Dom's emotions rushed through our new bond. I felt his regret and his ironclad determination.

But our bond went both ways, and I allowed him to feel my rage and hatred. "I will kill you," I promised.

A burst of agonizing pain drove me to my knees. I clutched my head in my hands, remembering too late my programming would automatically punish any aggression toward a handler.

Something that felt a lot like shame rippled through our bond. Dom offered me his hand.

Refusing to take it, I pushed myself to standing.

"You follow my orders now," he said, looking up at me.

I wanted more than anything to shift and slash that grim smugness off his face, but my programming forced me to bow my head to my new master. "I follow your orders."

"Tell me what happened to Sergeant Brooks?" Dom

demanded. I felt a flicker of something that might have been sadness coming from him.

"Sarge, the infected are almost on us," Darcy shouted from inside the vehicle.

Dom held up one finger.

"Is that Hunter?" she asked, peering out. "Is Jen here?"

Ignoring her, Dom repeated his question to me.

"Alpha Diaz of the Calaveras faction executed her at the urging of Dr. Hurran."

Dom clenched his fists, anger and pain seeping through our bond.

Maybe he'd cared for Jen after all.

"Why didn't you protect her?" Dom's tone wasn't accusatory, but it still stung.

"She didn't allow me to. She ordered me straight to you."

The rattling moans of the infected grew louder.

Dom straightened his shoulders. "I want a full report when we get back to base. Now make yourself invisible and clear our path to the school." Without waiting for a response, he jumped into the driver's seat and pulled the transport vehicle out into the street.

Bitterness filled me as I cloaked myself and followed his orders. I'd come so fucking close to having my freedom and everything I'd ever wanted, only to lose it all.

❧

BY THE TIME DOM PARKED THE TRANSPORT VEHICLE INSIDE the gates of a private school several miles away, I was drenched in blood. I'd taken out my rage on any infected who had the misfortune of stumbling close to the vehicle, and it showed.

As I tried to wipe my face clean with my hand, Dom

jumped out. "Wait next to the truck and don't interact with anyone, Hunter."

"Woof," I said automatically.

His lips twitched at my inside joke, but I felt hollow. Back when we were a team, I'd acted like a dog when I felt he was treating me like one. It normally resulted in him taking his commands down a notch. Not today.

Turning away from me, he stalked across the courtyard to speak with soldiers who were helping civilians off a bus.

Their conversation was lost on me the moment my mate climbed out of the transport vehicle.

Even wearing a shell-shocked expression and covered in blood she was stunning.

I physically ached with the need to touch her, but I settled for watching her shout at Darcy. "What are you doing? Don't you dare drop him."

My mate was such a bossy thing. I loved it.

"Shut your pie hole," Darcy replied, unceremoniously dumping Reed on the ground.

Lee cursed out Darcy while her sister jumped out of the truck and checked on Reed.

The cocksucker didn't look any worse for wear. In fact, between the two of us, he'd made out with the better deal.

My envy for the unconscious human grew as I watched Lee and Eden drag him toward the long line of men, women, and children waiting to enter the school. It took twenty minutes for them to make it inside, where I finally lost sight of them.

Dom seemed to have forgotten me. His attention bounced between his radio and the incoming and outgoing transport vehicles. Occasionally, he barked orders at the soldiers, most of which seemed to be Titans like himself. All of them seemed to be in a race against time.

To make space for the growing crowd of civilians, Darcy

moved the transport vehicle around to the side of the school. I had no choice but to walk next to the vehicle and wait while she parked it. She seemed unaware of my presence as she stalked back toward the front gates.

I wearily slumped against one of the back tires and faced my next dilemma. Dom had ordered me to cloak myself, however, it wasn't physically possible for me to hold that state for much longer. Once I became visible, my chip would automatically punish me for not following orders. In the old days, I would have brought this to Dom's attention, but now I'd rather let the pain kill me than ask for his mercy.

As I braced myself for the oncoming agony, my mind turned to my mate. I needed to see that she was okay. Throwing caution to the wind, I closed my eyes and pushed my consciousness out of my body.

Rising as an incorporeal mist, I flew around the school building where Dom stood with a radio pressed to his ear. "What do you mean evac isn't coming?" he shouted.

Although I couldn't feel his emotions in this disembodied state, seeing his mounting frustration filled me with grim satisfaction. It seemed we'd be at the school longer than he'd expected. Maybe much longer.

Mulling over the possible implications, I flew through the brick walls of the school. Then I traveled down a crowded hallway, past classrooms, and through a set of double doors that led to a gymnasium teeming with humans. Some huddled together on bleachers in the back, some sat on whatever belongings they'd brought with them, and some argued with the unfortunate soldiers trying to keep order.

Adding to the chaos were the half a dozen children racing from one end of the basketball court to the other, their joy a dark mirror to their parents' anxiety and fear.

Not finding my mate there, I searched adjacent rooms. The boys' locker room was empty, but a faint echo of voices drew me deeper inside the girls' locker room. I flew through the restroom stalls and lockers before finally finding Lee and her family in the shower area.

Reed lay on the white-tiled floor, a shirt bunched under his neck.

Eden, who was free of handcuffs and shackles, cleaned dried blood from his forehead. "Stop worrying, sissy. It's a mild concussion."

Lee, who was pacing back and forth under the shower-heads, whirled around. "I'm sorry, did I miss you getting your medical degree?"

Eden ignored my mate's sarcasm. "His pupils aren't dilated and his breathing and color look good. There's some bruising and swelling, but he'll be fine."

"You were a vet assistant, Edie. He needs to see a nurse or a doctor. There has to be someone in the gym that can help him." Lee started to walk out.

"Let me go," Eden said as she stood. "You'll scare the kids."

Lee frowned. "It's just a little blood."

"You're stanky, sissy."

"You're stankier," my mate shot back.

"Not possible. I'm going to grab some food from the vending machine before I start my doctor search, so you have time for a quick shower," Eden called out as she left the locker room.

Lee looked down at her bloody clothing and made a face. Then, giving Reed a quick glance, she walked to the open shower in the corner of the room and undressed.

Her bare skin drew me like a beacon. Transfixed, I floated next to her and watched her turn the water on.

She let out a muffled shriek when the icy spray hit her, and her nipples went stiff as berries. Berries, I longed to taste.

As the water turned steaming hot, tension seemed to

leave her shoulders. She found an abandoned bottle on the floor and began lathering herself down with its contents.

Seeing her hands move over her lush curves filled me with the need to reclaim every inch of her body.

Without even a flicker of indecision, I dove into Reed. I sensed the cocksucker attempting to regain consciousness, but it was easy enough to shove him aside and take control. A split-second later, I opened my new eyes and sat up. My head throbbed, but the dull pain was easy enough to ignore when my female was standing naked just a few feet away.

Lee faced the wall, her head under the streaming water. She didn't seem to hear me tear off the clothes I was wearing and pad barefoot over to her.

When I reached out to touch her back, she whirled around. Blinking furiously through the water running down her face, she said, "Thank God," and threw herself into my arms.

I groaned at how good her wet body felt pressed against me. My cock turned to stone and throbbed between us.

She jumped back, flushing. "Oh, um. You want to shower? I'm just finishing up."

"No, dirty dancer. I don't want to shower. I want to fuck you." I stepped under the showerhead. The spraying water made the cuts and bruises on my face sting like a bitch, but I ignored them. All my focus was on my mate.

She retreated until her back pressed against the wall. "Reed—"

"I'm not Reed," I said, bringing my mouth down on hers.

She gasped against my lips. Her hands pressed against my scarred chest as if to push me away, but then they twined around my neck. "We can't," she moaned against my lips. "Not here."

I deepened our kiss.

Her tongue danced with mine as my hands roamed her

slick skin. When I cupped her breast and thumbed her nipples, she broke our kiss to let out a ragged moan.

I scraped my mouth down her jaw and then lavished my attention on her incredible breasts.

Her breath came faster and sharper as I sucked her swollen nipples.

When I'd finally gotten my fill, I knelt down and laved her belly button ring with my tongue. The shiny piece of jewelry captivated me as much now as it had back in the club.

"Reed," she said again, the name sounding like a plea.

"Not Reed." Hot water scalded my back as I grabbed her leg and draped it over my shoulder.

Thrown off balance, she braced her hands against the wall. "What are you—?" Her question turned into a long moan when I buried my face between her legs.

Her sweet honey taste was so addictive. I'd licked her to three orgasms before the sound of a gasp had me jerking my head around.

Eden stood across the locker room wearing a shocked expression. "I—I'll be in the gym." With a squeak, she turned and ran.

"Oh, God." Lee closed her eyes and let the back of her head hit the wall. "She'll never let me hear the end of this."

"Let's make it worthwhile then." Giving her a wicked grin, I reclined back on the floor and yanked her down on top of me.

"Reed," she said breathlessly, her entrance poised over the tip of my cock.

"I told you. I'm not Reed." I gripped her hips and slammed up into her tight, wet heat.

She let out a hiss, her body trembling.

Fuck. She's probably sore from earlier. Cursing myself for being a brute, I went still. "We can stop." As much as I wanted her, I refused to bring her pain.

She caught her lower lip between her teeth and shook her head. Then she began to ride me. Initially, she moved slowly. Then, faster and faster. Soon her dizzying pace made my eyes cross and my balls ache with the need to spill inside her.

I fought for self-control, wanting to make our encounter last.

She made it near impossible with the way she circled her hips.

Keening sounds escaped her lips as her muscles tensed and her eyes went unseeing. Knowing she was close, I ground my pelvis against her clit.

She threw back her head and screamed so loud I imagined Dom could hear her orgasming outside.

A burst of masculine satisfaction rolled through me. "You're mine," I exclaimed.

Her spasming pussy clamped down so hard on me I saw stars. Unable to hold back, I came with a shout that echoed through the empty locker room.

Panting, Lee pushed her wet hair out of her face. "That was even better than last time, Not Reed."

Incapable of speaking, I grunted and dragged her over me. As I held her tightly under the hot spray of the shower, something that felt a lot like hope stirred inside my chest.

All was not lost. My twin brother was alive somewhere. I'd discovered a way to be with my mate. And although I was bound to my enemy, I'd found a way to slip his leash. Using this body, or another, I'd make Dom pay for his crimes.

Soon, I'd be free of him and anyone else who would seek to control me. Then, with my mate by my side, I'd make a new life in whatever remained of this world.

Ghost was right. Opportunity came from chaos and I was going to seize it by its motherfucking throat.

Smiling against my mate's wet hair, I let myself relax for the first time in a very long time.

"Sooo," a voice drawled inside my head. "Am I still hallucinating?"

⁂

The adventure continues with Claiming Her Beasts Book Two (keep reading for a preview)

THE CITY FELL. HELP NEVER CAME. NOW OUR LIVES depend on playing by Dominic's punishing rules. But the icy-cold sergeant's brutal tactics and questionable motives make him just as dangerous as the monsters outside.

EVEN WORSE, MY VISCERAL ATTRACTION TO DOMINIC AND a deadly shifter is pushing Reed further into insanity. His bouts of amnesia and animalistic rages may force me to make a soul-shattering choice—love or survival?

ABOUT THE AUTHOR

Dia wanted to be a writer from the time she could hold a pencil. A lover of paranormal romance, reverse harem, science fiction, urban fantasy, and horror, she writes action-packed stories featuring kick-butt heroines and the alpha male heroes who fall for them.

You can find her books on amazon.

If you want to be notified when the next book in the series releases please sign up for my newsletter.

You can follow Dia on:
https://diacole.com/
or
Join her reader group:
https://www.facebook.com/groups/1082971415136332

BOOKS BY DIA COLE

CLAIMING HER MATES

Claiming The Nanny

Claiming Her Mates: Book One

Claiming Her Mates: Book Two

Claiming Her Mates: Book Three

Claiming Her Mates Series Collection

CLAIMING HER BEASTS

Claiming Her Beasts: Book One

Claiming Her Beasts: Book Two

Claiming Her Beasts: Book Three

Claiming Her Beasts: Book Four

CLAIMING HER CONSORTS

Claiming the Wardens

EXCERPT FROM CLAIMING HER BEASTS: BOOK TWO

❧ 1 ❧

REED

I woke to find the woman I loved lying naked on top of me. Even more mind-blowing, I was inside her.

Holy shit! I'd give anything to remember how we got to this point. Rubbing my aching head, I glanced around. With the warm water spraying down on us and the lockers running the length of the room around us we had to be in a locker room.

How did we get here?

Lee's wet hair tickled my nose as she nestled her cheek in the hollow of my breastbone. She let out a contented sigh. "I want to stay with you like this forever."

My chest tightened at her words even though I knew it wasn't real. None of this was real. Lee would never cuddle with me, much less have sex with me. Despite us not being related, she still treated me as if I were a younger brother.

I must still be hallucinating. My best friend, Ronnie, had roofied me at my twentieth birthday party last night. I'd been on one hell of a trip ever since then.

First, I'd fantasized that Lee let me go down on her before some ten-foot monster with glowing eyes barged into her room. Then we'd apparently had sex for the first time shortly before our best friends turned into zombies and attacked us. After I'd beat their brains out and acted as the getaway driver for Lee's sister's jailbreak, badass gang members showed up at our house and beat the crap out of me.

And just the other day Ronnie said I lacked creativity. Just wait until I told him about this crazy ass hallucination.

"This isn't a hallucination, cocksucker," a strange voice rumbled in my mind. *"But do us both a favor and go back to sleep."*

Jesus. I'm hearing voices now. Whatever crap Ronnie had given me must have been really strong.

What if I can't wake up from it? My heart pounded.

Ronnie's cousin was once hospitalized for drug-induced psychosis that lasted weeks.

Shit.

"We really should join the others, Not Reed," Lee said, rising over me. Her deep chocolate eyes were slumberous, and her long, hip-length brown hair looked almost black under the spray of the shower.

So captivated by the water running down the slopes of her beautiful breasts it took me a moment to focus on her words. *Why is she calling me Not Reed?*

"She's talking to me," answered the voice in my head.

All at once, the alien presence shoved me to the back recesses of my mind. There I found myself unable to move my body, but still fully aware of everything that was happening to me. Or, more specifically, the things I was doing to Lee.

In one of the most disconcerting moments of my life, I experienced myself leaning up and clamping my lips around one of Lee's nipples.

Her husky moan rang in my ears.

Dazed, I felt my teeth bite down. *Jesus.* That had to hurt.

Lee didn't seem in pain, though. She threw her head back with a wild cry and rocked on my hardening cock.

Whatever controlled my body, gripped her hips and yanked her off my shaft. Then it roughly positioned her on her hands and knees.

"You look so fucking beautiful, dirty dancer," I heard myself say as the entity shoved her thighs apart and knelt behind her on the wet tile.

I couldn't disagree. Lee looked like a goddess with her breasts heaving and her legs splayed. The glistening pink flesh between her toned thighs was the most erotic thing I'd ever seen.

My pierced cock was slowly fed into her.

Jesus. I'd imagined being with Lee all my life, but none of those fantasies came close to this. The sensation of entering her hot, wet pussy was indescribable. Overcome with lust, I forgot about being a bystander and lost myself in the thrill of being inside her.

She moaned and swiveled her hips. "Oh, God. Your barbells, Reed. They're amazing."

I felt a rush of masculine pride. I'd endured the pain of those piercings for her pleasure alone and I'd go through it all again just to hear the music of her husky moans.

"Not Reed," the entity controlling me growled. He grabbed her hair and yanked her head back so fast her teeth snapped together.

"Don't hurt her!" I mentally shouted. But the entity ignored me.

Lee's eyes blazed with fury. "Let go of my hair, *Reed.*"

That's my girl. Lee would let no one, including me, manhandle her.

The entity released her hair, reached around her and pinched her nipple. "What's my name?"

Lee inhaled sharply. "Stop these games, Reed."

"Wrong answer." The entity slipped a hand between her legs and pinched her clit. "What's my name?"

She tried to move away, but my hands gripped her hips forcing her in place.

"Stop hurting her!" I struggled to take control of my body.

"Not Reed," Lee gasped.

"Good." The body snatcher shoved her face to the floor and slammed balls deep inside her. So deep, I swear I could feel her damn cervix.

She let out a broken cry.

The entity hammered into her with deep, savage thrusts.

"Please! Please!" she pleaded over the wet slapping sounds of our bodies.

Lee never begged for anything. I couldn't stand to see the woman I loved so abused.

A rush of white-hot rage gave me the strength to regain control. I immediately jerked myself out of her.

Panting, Lee glanced over her shoulder. "Don't you dare stop."

"Y-you liked that?" I asked, stunned.

"Of course she liked it, cocksucker," that alien voice roared in my mind.

"Go away! Stop talking to me!" I shouted.

Lee twisted all the way around, an expression of outrage on her face.

I held up my hand in an apology. "I didn't mean you, honey. There's someone else talking to me." I tapped the side of my head.

"The name is Hunter."

Lee's irritated look morphed into an expression of concern. "Are you okay?"

"Yes. No. I don't know." I rubbed the painful egg-sized lump on the side of my head. "I don't know what's real and what's not." I had to be hallucinating. But everything felt so real. The pain in my head. The wet spray of the water on my bruised face. The fierce throbbing ache of my cock.

Lee reached up to turn off the shower. As soon as the water cut off, she knelt beside me. "Those gang members really knocked you around."

"But I got some good punches in first, right?" I tried to smile, but only managed to split my lip. The stinging pain added to my growing feeling of discomfort. I hated showing anyone the disfiguring scars on my chest and here I sat naked and exposed in front of her.

"She doesn't care," Hunter interjected. I didn't like that the body snatcher could read my thoughts.

Hunter made a sound of exasperation. *"Of course I can read your thoughts. I'm in your fucking mind."*

"Go away!" I pleaded.

"Reed..." Lee stopped and corrected herself. "Not Reed."

I waved my hand. "Reed is fine."

"Fuck you," groused Hunter.

Lee chewed her bottom lip. "I should have told you earlier that you weren't hallucinating. All of it was real. Ronnie and Cami. The gang members. The apocalypse." She licked her lips. "Us."

I could only shake my head. "No." There was no way. It was too fantastical. Too improbable.

"Listen to her, cocksucker."

Lee looked down at her feet. Like everything else about her, they were perfect. Although I was more of a boob guy, I had to admire how sexy her toenails look painted in that glittery black polish.

"Focus. My mate is talking to you," Hunter snarled.

"Shut up," I muttered back. "She's not your mate."

Lee let out a heavy sigh. "This is my fault. If I'd been straight with you, you never would have charged Javier's men like that. It was suicidal."

I blinked. *Who's Javier?*

"The gang leader. Try to keep up," Hunter admonished.

"Stop it! Just stop talking to me!" I shouted out loud.

Lee reared back.

"You're fucking this up. Let me take over."

I was suddenly hurled into the recesses of my mind. Helpless, I could only observe as Hunter used my body to grab Lee. "So where were we, dirty dancer?"

She pulled away. "Reed, you're scaring me."

"I'm not Reed. Let's finish what we started." Hunter, grabbed my cock and pumped it several times to stiffen it.

Enraged and feeling horribly violated, I mentally shouted, *"Get the fuck out!"* Then I retook control of my body and forced myself to stand. "Lee, stay away from me. There is someone... something inside me. It wants you."

"She's my fucking mate, of course I want her," Hunter shouted. *"She wants me, too."*

"No! She doesn't want you. Leave her alone." My breath came in shallow pants.

Lee's eyes widened, and she stumbled back. "Okay, just calm down." She ran over to a pile of blood-spattered clothes and yanked them on.

"Congratulations, asshole. She's getting dressed."

"Get out of my head!" I slapped my forehead hard enough to make my ears ring.

Hunter went silent for several heartbeats. Just when I thought he'd gone away, he snarled. *"Why don't you get out? I like this body. I'm going to keep it."*

"No, you're not." Turning, I rammed my head against the tile wall. Stars burst across my line of vision and for a blessed moment, that voice quieted.

Lee made a choking sound. "I-I'm going to get you some help."

I hated that I was freaking her out, but I needed her to

leave. "Go," I said, wiping the blood from my nose. "Stay away from me."

In a shocking show of strength, Hunter wrestled control away from me again. "Ignore him. Come back to me, my dirty dancer."

I regained control just in time to stop Hunter from following her out of the room. "No, you don't." Not knowing what else to do, I drove my skull into the closest metal locker.

Bang.

Pain exploded inside my head, along with a wave of dizziness that brought me to my knees. Blood filled my mouth and ran down the back of my throat.

A full minute of silence passed.

Thank Jesus. It worked. Holding my head in my hands, I slowly staggered to my feet.

Hunter chuckled. *"That won't stop me, cocksucker."* Then he took control again.

"Dirty dancer!" I heard myself shout. Helpless, I could only watch as we stumbled out of the locker room and into a gymnasium filled with people.

Dozens of unfamiliar faces gawked at the sight of me. I must have looked like something straight out of a horror movie with my long hair tangled over my bloody face and the scarred mess of my upper body on display.

Most of the women, and several of the men, weren't staring at my face though. They gaped at all the metal running the length of my semi-hard dick.

Fuck no. Being exposed like this in front of so many people was my worst nightmare. But I was helpless to do anything to stop Hunter from plowing through the throngs of people. "Dirty dancer! Get back here!"

A soldier stepped into my path. "Put your clothes on, Hippie."

Holy Shit. The guy looked exactly like my childhood G.I. Joe action figure come to life. Not only did he have biceps bigger than my head, he was equipped with enough weapons to arm a small country.

Hunter didn't seem impressed. "Go fuck yourself, Dom." He tried to shove the man mountain out of our way. When the soldier didn't budge an inch. Hunter balled my hand into a fist and swung at him.

G.I. Joe caught the punch, clenched his powerful hand around mine, and threw my fist back into my face so hard I flew into the air.

People scrambled out of the way as I crashed down. My head slammed against the wood floor with a thwack and everything went dark.

DID YOU ENJOY THIS PREVIEW OF CLAIMING HER BEASTS: BOOK TWO?

You can find it available on amazon.

EXCERPT FROM CLAIMING HER MATES: BOOK ONE

❦ I ❦

HAVANA

"What do you want for Christmas, you naughty girl?" asked the middle-aged man leering at me. The light from the dusty chandelier reflected off the gold band on his left hand, temporarily blinding me.

He probably told his wife he was working late. Ugh. Years of playing my seductive role prevented me from curling my lip in disdain. Instead, I continued undulating to the beat of the dance music being piped into the small red velvet VIP room.

"Come on, you can tell me," the man insisted, stroking his Santa-like white beard.

I should've been coy with my answer, but the truth sprang from my lips before I could bite back the words. "Someone to share it with."

The man blinked up at me with blood-shot eyes.

Great, Vana, why don't you just kill the mood? Trying to salvage the moment, I tossed back my hip-length black hair and winked playfully. "Is that someone you?" With a practiced flick of my fingers, I slowly removed my silver-studded black top and tossed it to the man.

He tried to catch it and missed. The tiny scrap of material

slithered to the blood-red carpet as he fixed his gaze on my swaying bare breasts.

"Have you been a bad boy this year?"

"Y-yes," he stammered. His eyes glazed over as he swayed in his seat.

He must be trashed. Good. A drunk and his money are soon parted. Throwing club rules out the window, I stepped down from the small raised platform I was dancing on and approached his chair. "Then you need to be punished."

"Yes, Mistress Robin," he gasped. Unlike most of the club patrons intrigued by my dominatrix persona, this one seemed truly snared by the fantasy. For the right price, I was happy to indulge him.

I cast a furtive glance at the camera nestled at the base of the chandelier. In the past, Max, the club owner, might've skinned me alive if he'd caught me doing a little extra on the side. Now he'd only ask for a percentage.

Times were tough for everyone. Strip clubs included. Case in point, this guy managed to secure a private dance from me for a mere seventy bucks, something that would've been unheard of before the canine flu hit this past spring. But global pandemics had a way of changing things.

I leaned over the man, my nipples grazing his rumpled tweed vest. "It'll cost you."

"I have money." He reached into his olive dress pants pocket and pulled out a worn leather wallet with trembling hands. "How much?"

I arched an eyebrow. "How much do you have?"

He opened his wallet and out fluttered several receipts.

Sadly, it looked like he had only a handful of twenties, but it was better than going home broke. "That works," I purred. I wouldn't have sex with him, of course, but men like him weren't after that anyway. Years ago, my mom explained some men get off as much on pain and humiliation as they did pleasure. Ah, the joys of having a stripper mom. While other kids were learning how to ride bikes, Mom was giving me crash courses in the various ways to seduce men. Big surprise I ended up at the same club where she used to work.

The man swallowed hard, sweat dripping off him as if he was in a sauna. "Take it all." He pushed his wallet at me.

I found myself staring at a family photo. Gathered in the arms of a heavyset woman were three young children. I couldn't help glancing between the professor and the photo. *Why isn't he home with them?* Hell, if I'd had kids there's no way I wouldn't be with them right now. With a pang, I remembered the big amber eyes of the little girl I'd used to nanny for. *I miss Mira so much...*

Her father's handsome face flashed in my mind and my throat tightened. It'd been three months since Nathan shattered my heart, but the pain was still fresh. Trying to put my ex out of my mind, I flipped past the photo and found the twenties. Mentally tallying the money, I pulled out the folded bills and slid them into the top of my thigh-high stiletto boot. A genuine smile tugged at the corner of my lips, it was a better haul than I'd anticipated. "Take off your clothes, Dr. Sullivan."

He gaped at me for a moment.

I tossed his wallet back at him not bothering to explain that I'd seen his Southern Arizona University ID badge inside. "I said, take off your clothes. Now."

He jumped to his feet. "Yes, Mistress Robin." He gazed up at me adoringly.

My five-foot-ten height plus my seven-inch stilettos ensured I towered over nearly everyone I encountered, including the professor.

He fumbled with the top buttons of his oxford shirt before realizing he needed to remove his vest first.

"Fold your clothes and place them over there," I

instructed, pointing at the side table that in better days held ice buckets filled with Cristal. Now a bottle of drugstore champagne swam in a plastic tub of melted ice.

He practically tore off his vest and shirt. As he unbuckled his belt, he turned to face me. "I've never done this before."

I made a noncommittal noise. *Right. That's what they all say.* Finally noticing his bare torso, I inhaled sharply. *What the hell?* Black veins covered the man's flabby arms and a portion of his silver-haired chest. I'd seen some strange-looking tattoos over the years, but nothing like that. Unable to help myself, I asked, "What's going on there?"

The man looked down and paled. "My God. Those weren't there this morning." He gave me a frantic look as if I had the answers.

I backed up a step studying his bloodshot eyes, pale skin, and sweaty face with new eyes. *He's not just drunk.* "You're sick." And that meant I needed to get as far away from him as possible. I'd never heard of the canine flu causing dark veins like that, but you don't mess around with a bug that killed a quarter of the world's population.

He raised his hands. "I'm not. I just got the canine flu vaccine yesterday," he said, mentioning the coveted shots the CDC had just rolled out. "I-I don't feel so good." His knees buckled, and he fell back into his chair.

Shit. "I'll get help." *Max will know what to do.* I turned to grab the curtain.

"No. My wife. She can't find out..." he gasped sliding to the floor.

Damn. If the guy passed out in my VIP room, I'd never hear the end of it from the other girls. Especially Jess. That nasty redhead would love to get one over on me. She'd been downright venomous since I reported one of her stupid pranks to Max. *Who the hell coats the stage steps with baby oil? Seriously.* I'd taken a nasty fall and probably fractured my spine, not that I could afford to get my aching back looked at by a doctor.

"Please, don't call Sharon," the professor wheezed bringing my focus back to him.

"No one will call your wife. Just relax. I'll be right back." I bent down, retrieved my top and tied it back on.

He nodded, flashing me a relieved look.

I blinked. *Are more of his veins darkening?* Shuddering, I pushed through the heavy velvet curtain door and rushed down a long hallway back into the main club. Immediately I was assaulted by the smell of liquor, cigarette smoke, and the twang of the latest hit country single. On the stage, the new girl, Jade, twirled around the pole in a cowboy hat and crotchless chaps. *Poor girl,* I thought with a stab of sympathy. Max had wanted me to cover Jess's country set after she was a no-show for the second time this week, but I'd talked him into having the new girl do it. Good experience and all. Seeing her dance to a sea of empty tables filled me with guilt. No one even watched. Sly, one of the regulars, was already passed out and the group of dark-haired men sitting in the back of the club ignored her.

As if feeling my gaze, one of the heavily tattooed men looked up at me. He gave me a once-over and flashed me a dazzling set of gold teeth. The long-haired man sitting next to him followed his friend's gaze and leered at me with a predatory intensity that made me glad for the knife hidden in my boot. A girl couldn't be too careful these days.

I bit back a shiver of fear as the long-haired man beckoned me over. Their gang, the Calaveras, was one of the deadliest in Arizona and I needed their kind of attention like I needed an engineering degree. Ignoring the men and their menacing vibe, I scanned the rest of the near empty club for Max.

He was at the bar, eyes glued to the television along with

Donna, the cocktail waitress, and Justin, the gray-haired bartender who looked like he'd been a defensive lineman back in the day. I'd always wondered why he had a television at his bar. *I mean who comes to a strip club to watch TV?*

Donna looked up as I approached. "Honey, you need to see this. There's some freaky shit going down." She ran a hand through her bleach blond hair, knocking aside the felt Santa hat she was wearing.

I shook my head. "Tell me about it. I got a guy covered in black veins about to pass out in the VIP room."

"What?" Max jerked his bald head up so fast his jowls shook.

"We might need to call an ambulance." I waited for Max to make an obscene joke, but instead a panicked expression crossed his face.

"You said his veins were black?"

I nodded.

Donna let out a gasp. "The news reporter said to watch out for people with dark veins. Some folks are having bad reactions to the canine flu vaccine. They're getting sick and..." she lowered her voice, "turning into cannibals."

I gave her an incredulous look. "What?"

"See for yourself." She waved at the television hanging above a tower of colorful liquor bottles.

On the screen a flustered news reporter was babbling. "Reports of violent behavior in some of the recently vacci-nated are coming in from all across the country."

The program cut to a clip of dazed-looking people in hospital gowns attacking a young man on the street. The jerky footage must've been taken on someone's cell phone. Whoever was holding the phone kept repeating, "Holy shit," over and over while the crowd literally tore the screaming man to pieces.

My stomach churned as I watched the deranged crowd

gulp down handfuls of the man's flesh. "That's horrible. I can't believe they showed that on television."

Donna shook her head. "It's not just happening here. It's happening all over the world. They rushed the flu vaccine to market without doing the proper tests and now it's turning people into monsters. Oh, God. And just an hour ago I was cursing the fact that they didn't have the vaccine available for Gavin." She let out a sob at the mention of her son who'd died of the flu earlier in the year.

"Don't cry, muffin," Max said in a gruff voice. He slung one beefy arm around Donna's thin shoulder and gave me a hard look. "Get that sick guy out of here. Now." He used his don't-argue-with-me voice.

That tone hadn't worked on me since I'd been ten. "But Max—"

He interrupted me. "I'll call him a cab. You get him in it. We're closing early tonight. Donna, go get Sly up. I'll tell Mr. Diaz and his men that they need to leave." He looked over at the dark-haired men in back and shuddered. "Let's hope they don't kill me," he muttered under his breath as he headed over to their table.

I'd take the sick professor over throwing deadly gang members out of the club any day. As I turned to walk back to the VIP area, Donna called my name softly.

I spun around to see that the older woman wore an anxious expression on her face.

She smoothed an invisible wrinkle from her short black skirt. "Honey, I'm sorry but Max and I won't be able to make your Christmas Eve dinner."

"Oh," I said, trying not to let my disappointment show. *You and everyone else.* "That's too bad."

"We're sorry to miss it, it's just that with everything going on..." She waved weakly at the television set. "And it's our first Christmas without Gavin." Her voice hitched.

"I understand." I reached over and hugged her. I missed that kid something fierce. Pushing the memory of the mischievous little boy out of my mind before I started tearing up too, I looked over at Justin. "You and Sam are still coming, right?"

The big guy shook his head. "Sorry, sweetheart. Sam just wants to do a family thing this year." He gave me an apologetic smile.

Family thing. Right. "Well, more turkey for me," I said, hiding my misery with a smile. "Have a good night."

Donna and Justin waved as I headed back toward the professor. My chest tightened. Bad enough that the anniversary of my mother's death was Christmas Eve. Now I'd have to endure it alone.

The wail of country music faded as I moved past the stage and through the long, deserted hallway. I stopped at the closed velvet curtain to the room where I'd left the professor. A low moaning sound came from inside. "Dr. Sullivan?" I reached out to pull open the curtain and hesitated. I'd never realized how far from the main club this area was. *What if the professor is sick like the people on TV? What if he attacks me?*

DID YOU ENJOY THIS PREVIEW OF CLAIMING HER MATES: BOOK ONE?

You can find it available on amazon.

Please don't forget to leave a review if you enjoyed this work!

Thank you for reading!